Advance praise for *A*

2020

"A resolute deep dive into an inner s
and a timely reminder that there's an entire universe inside of everyone
we meet. You will be moved."

—Matthew Quick, *New York Times* bestselling
author of *The Silver Linings Playbook*

"*A Room Called Earth* offers a strikingly unique look at intimacy, identity, and time itself. From now on I want every novel to be this fiercely authentic, this assured, this untethered from the status quo. Madeleine Ryan is a wholly original writer; this debut announces a tremendous talent."

—Kimberly King Parsons, National Book Award
nominated author of *Black Light*

"In prose filled with humor and warm light, Madeleine Ryan unearths the bright, luminous soul of each animate and inanimate being she encounters. Instead, remarkably, it is the self shaped by and against social norms that is met as an other. The result is an intelligence that feels not only totally refreshing and original but wonderfully humane."

—Meng Jin, author of *Little Gods*

"I have never read anything like *A Room Called Earth* before, and I'm sure I never will again. In this precious gemstone of a novel, Ryan communicates a lush, raw, addictive truth with her prosaic yet theatrical prose, her protagonist witnessing the world in a way that had me pausing for long deep breaths after most chapters. The world of this book is the world of a woman who knows herself because she has needed to, and a woman who many might recognize, despite her oneness. Reading Ryan is to be taught and to be refreshed, and I will return to her pages in the future, to remind me of the beauty there is in my own room called earth."

—Laura McPhee Browne, author of *Cherry Beach*

"A daring, prismatic novel about seeing and being seen, and the hunger for universal connection. Madeleine Ryan's clarity of vision imbues the ordinary—a party, strangers, inner-city streets—with cosmic significance. I came out of *A Room Called Earth* with fresh eyes and a full heart."

—Laura Elizabeth Woollett, author of *Beautiful Revolutionary*

"Madeleine Ryan's *A Room Called Earth* heralds the debut of a writer to whom it is worth attending. Flashes of insight, eruptions of startling descriptions, and an original style all add to the excitement of discovering Ryan's fresh observations of the world around her protagonist. Worth reading slowly to savor this highly engaging perspective and this unique new voice."

—Naomi Wolf, author of *Outrages: Sex, Censorship, and the Criminalization of Love*

"An honest narration of human experience and how our whirling minds perceive the world. Sensual, raw, real, and down to earth."

—Katie Hess, author of *Flowerevolution*

"Vibrant and revealing. Ryan succeeds in capturing neurodiversity on the page."

—*Publishers Weekly*

"The narrator's voice is astute, clear, and strong as the vodka she likes, as luminous as sparkling stars. Madeleine Ryan has created a marvelous woman and a joyous story."

—Shelf Awareness

PENGUIN BOOKS

A ROOM CALLED EARTH

Madeleine Ryan is an Australian writer, director, and author. Her articles and essays have appeared in SBS, *The Daily Telegraph*, *The Sydney Morning Herald*, *Vice*, *Bustle*, *Lenny Letter*, and *The New York Times*, and she is currently working on the screen adaptation of *A Room Called Earth*. Madeleine lives in rural Victoria.

A Room Called Earth

Madeleine Ryan

PENGUIN
BOOKS

PENGUIN BOOKS
An imprint of Penguin Random House LLC
penguinrandomhouse.com

ISBN 9780143135456 (paperback)
ISBN 9780525507123 (ebook)

Printed in the United States of America
1 3 5 7 9 10 8 6 4 2

Designed by Alexis Farabaugh

for the hearts of our fathers

A Room Called Earth

1.

I decided to wear a kimono and high heels to the party because I wanted people to see me in a kimono and high heels at the party. I tried putting chopsticks from the kitchen drawer in my hair and it felt like it was overdoing things a bit, so I put them back. I even considered painting the chopsticks black because they were brown, and black would have suited my outfit better. Yet the fact that I considered painting them at all caused me to be embarrassed at myself, so I decided to ditch accessories that were at one time used to stuff pad Thai into someone's face. Painted or not, you can't change the reality of what chopsticks are or the main way that they've been used for, like, centuries. Eons, even. So let a chopstick be a chopstick, and my hair can be what it is, too.

I've fantasized for days about wearing this kimono and these shoes, and tonight is the night. The shoes are high and patent and black and shiny, and the kimono is red and silky with sleeves like wings. I guess the sleeves are a part of a traditional style, or whatever. It's just that my only association with them is that they're like wings. I don't know why they're so wide, or if that has some kind of practical aspect to it, and, you know, who cares.

I've put a tight black spandex skirt underneath for modesty. Well, it's a half-hearted gesture in the direction of modesty. I'm not wearing underwear of any kind because that would be ridiculous.

The people who are going to see this outfit and me in it are both known and unknown to me. I mean, I've been invited to this party. Like, I'm legitimately allowed to be there. It's just that my self-image is in no way going to be constrained by knowing too many people in attendance. I won't be readily identifiable to the majority of the crowd, so who and what I am can remain undefined, and expansive.

And, right now, from my perspective, the people who are going to be there are made up of Futuristic Shadow Beasts Without Faces that are deeply impressed by me. They make life worth living, because I can decide exactly who and what they are, from this place of having no actual idea. I can just imagine them, and dress for them, and have high expectations of them, and envisage the amazing connections that I might have with them. And I hope that all of the Futuristic Shadow Beasts Without Faces are currently giving themselves the same rapturous, pre-party experience that I am. Because even if we don't get a chance to meet, or to talk, we can remain in a state of wonderment together. My dream is to leave people wondering, and nothing more. It's safe, it's sexy, and I want to live there forever.

Mystery is my favorite accessory.

As I get ready, I keep looking over my shoulder just in case someone walks into the room unannounced. My music is loud, and I'm worried that someone will knock and I won't be made aware of their presence until it's too late, and who knows what they will have witnessed or, worse, how they'll perceive what they have witnessed. I don't even want to think about it.

It's one thing to be humiliated for my own reasons and a whole other thing to be the catalyst for someone else's sense of humiliation. I really don't want to take on that responsibility. I've always felt a strong inclination to smooth things over for the people around me, and now I've become terrified of the prospect of having to do so at all. I'm not really wired to care for other people unless they ask me directly because, in any given situation, I'm either completely immersed in myself, or completely immersed in someone else. There's no in-between.

Anyway. I keep sensing footsteps down the hallway and it's fucking annoying. They're echoing around my rib cage, and, I mean, no one ever walks in. How did I get to a point where I feared that they might? Every strand of hair is standing on end and my neck is moving like a magnet toward the door. Why? Is it self-obsession? Paranoia? Anxiety? My inner processes can be visceral to the point of being completely illusory, and absurd. Thankfully I live with a cat called Porkchop who is a very grounding influence upon me.

Porkchop is ginger and his job is to sit on my bed and stare at me, and he's very good at it. It was a self-appointed position, and he never lets the team down. I once read in a book that we need to be wary of growing too close to animals, because it can reveal a lack of closeness with our own species, and, around the same time, a boyfriend read aloud a section of a novella, which said that people who empathize with the animals involved in bullfighting don't empathize with human beings—like, at all—and that they're more likely to be psychopaths. We were in his kitchen when he shared this with me, and I remember taking a deep breath, from my shoulders, and quietly mashing more clumps out of the guacamole.

Connection with my own species has been difficult. I'm more at ease with the animal part of myself than the human part of myself. I feel at peace when I'm with Porkchop. I have no concerns about what he might or might not be thinking, or what might or might not happen next. Porkchop is always clear about his wants and needs. They aren't hidden behind lies, or delusions. They're right there, in the sunlight, wanting a tummy rub. Or, they very obviously prefer tuna to sardines, because the sardines are left on the plate and the tuna isn't. Or, they've carefully positioned the ball of string at the bottom of the stairs, because it's playtime.

Porkchop and I access a sense of wholeness that I rarely experience anywhere, or with anyone else. Our non-verbal union re-creates the stillness of the respective wombs we left long ago. We can't be all that different, really, because we pretty much came from the same place, and now we're here, living in the same place, and one day, we'll die, and end up in the same place.

Porkchop must feel the same way, because he doesn't go anywhere. That cat barely moves due to being so overcome with contentment in our space together. Everything that he does, and every sound that he makes, and every bit of smoked salmon that he licks, and carefully chews, suggests the utmost confidence in his decision-making capabilities. I see no reason to question Porkchop's level of commitment. I can trust the satisfaction that he experiences at my side, because when people or things want to move on, they just do.

Porkchop is also a potent reminder of why I don't eat anything like, or associated with, pork chops. I look at Porkchop and I feel safe in the knowledge that I don't eat his kind, or take what wasn't given to me by his kind. Porkchop isn't a sandwich, and he doesn't belong on a barbecue. He's a cat, and he lives with me. Just like all of the animals living alongside humans everywhere, every day, all the time, at every corner of the earth. Not just in houses or on farms. They're in the sea, and in the air, and in the jungles, and rainforests, and in the native parklands, and in all of the other places that animals are, which is heaps and heaps of places. We've all ended up here together, and that's all there is to it, because that's all the knowledge that we have about it.

Symbolically, Porkchop is "every animal" to me and I love him dearly. Look at him. He has a little soul, which has an agenda that miraculously involves staring at me all day. I feel so blessed.

Sometimes when he sits on my lap, I tell him that he's a god, and he shuts his eyes with what I'm sure is a gentle, appreciative knowing. We're all gods, and the ancient Egyptians withheld from those who refused to accept that.

An ex-boyfriend once said that I should "stop trying to be Holly Golightly" with my cat, and I said that he should stop relating everything back to the first pop-culture reference that pops into his head, because it won't make him any more relevant or useful to the tribe. And relating me to a man-made fantasy of womanhood said more about him than it did about me. He's in advertising now where he belongs, and we spent a year together that I don't really think about unless I'm talking to my therapist.

2.

I like to sip vodka martinis with olives before I go out, because Dad used to make a vodka martini with olives for Mum every night before dinner. It was their evening ritual. After a long day of writing and researching, he'd put on Artie Shaw and roll out a bowl of pistachios. Mum would put her feet up on the coffee table, snap the shells open with her long, pale-pink nails, and suck the salt off, before taking a sip of the brew and crunching a nut.

Dad took a lot of pride in the fact that he made the strongest martinis anyone in his circle of friends had ever drunk. Grown men were often seen keeling over on the lawn outside after a few of Dad's martinis. He never drank them himself.

Vodka martinis with olives are a family tradition that I've chosen to celebrate and embrace. There's something very decadent and straight-to-the-point about a vodka martini with olives. There's no yeast or citrus or bubbles to be used as a distraction. And I like to experience life directly and intimately so, naturally, I like to drink alcohol that is direct and intimate. Drinking vodka in this way, you get to feel every bit of it. There's no hiding from a vodka martini with olives.

Gin doesn't taste the same, or have the same feel about it, and I'm not sure why. Vodka is cold and clear, and it hits the bottom of my stomach like an ax, so, sorry to the guy I once dated who liked gin with soda and cucumber in it, it's just that that's a completely different thing. My family's martinis don't have a drop of gin in them, and there's nothing more to be said about that subject because it will get boring.

3.

I used to get ready to go out with other girls because that's what girls are supposed to do and it's meant to be all *Grease* without the bullying, except the bullying is always there. That's why Sandra Dee ends up singing about Danny outside by herself, next to a play pool, in a white nightie. And if you looked at my best friend and me during high school, you'd think I was Rizzo and she was Sandra Dee, and that would be a misconception. Maybe every woman thinks that would be a misconception.

My hair was long, thick, brown, and wavy, and hers was white-blond and straight. My hair looked different depending on the weather, and on how I had slept, and on how I had chosen to wear it the day before, and on what I had been thinking about too much, and hers was always the same. Like, exactly the same. Even after she washed it. She would try to cut it in different ways to create variation, yet every layer would remain visible and readily identifiable.

Try as she might to embrace unpredictability, her very being refused it. She did everything she could to rail against sameness and monotony. She moved across the landscape of life like a lightning rod: fast, primed, and ready for the next destination to electrify with her presence. She always had a bag in hand or over a shoulder in preparation for leaving. Her sky-blue eyes would rapidly assess situations, and people, before turning their attention back to a heavily distorted body image, which would shriek at her from every mirror and shop-window reflection.

During summer at the beach, I would play in the shallows like a mermaid and read novels filled with sand, as she chased surf-lifesaver boys past the break and inhaled freshly made salad sandwiches in front of them. The act of eating and nourishing herself was a spectator sport for the benefit of men and boys only. Eating like that always required an audience, because it was a public testament to a degree of normalcy that she practiced nowhere else. She never ate with such gusto when we were alone together or, if she did, it became swaddled in a sense of guilt so palpable that we both suffocated.

It was easy to get caught up in the swell of her energy, and expectations. I have an extraordinary capacity to be taken way out of my depth by the desires of others, and I'll never forget the time I tried to chase her chasing the surf-lifesaver boys past the break and I was dunked repeatedly. The tide knew exactly what the fuck was up, and it knew how to say it to me without tentativeness or restraint.

Stop.

She loved going to parties with me because her body had a lot more to say to the opposite sex than I did. Her big cheekbones, and white-blond hair, and large breasts made for very engaging conversation. Yet she often became fed up with the limitations of this. She wanted to be seen as more than a plaything. So she would try and beat the boys at drinking games I didn't want to have anything to do with, and she would crack sex jokes that I didn't understand.

I lived poetry and she lived politics. When she lost her virginity, it was because she wanted to get it over with, and when I lost mine, it was because the stars were bright, and I was infatuated.

One night she had a dream about sprinting against a group of other women in order to "win" the affections of a guy that she had set her sights upon. She awoke from the dream, arrived at brunch, ordered a soy latte and scrambled eggs on sourdough, and asked me what it meant. As her loyal soothsayer, I gently said that it seemed to reflect the ways in which she allowed the whims of men to dictate the parameters of her existence, and that she obviously saw herself as being in competition with other women. She looked at me, smiled, and said nothing. She enjoyed being seen, regardless of what other people saw. I admired that about her.

She won't be at the party tonight because she's already married to a mortgage, two dogs, two cars, one baby, another on the way, a man without a job who golfs on Saturdays, and a large plasma-screen TV that stays on in the background when you go to spend time with her. And I've never been able to find a suitable pre-party replacement. Because while she was busy chasing surf-lifesaver boys, and sprinting against other girls, she won my heart, and she still has it.

4.

These days I prepare to go out on my own. Well, technically, it's on my own. It never feels like it, though. Everything comes alive when I'm technically by myself.

Earlier tonight, I started the festivities in the bathtub. I soaked in warm water with Epsom salts, and castor oil, and vitamin C, and diatomaceous earth, and bush flower essences, and bicarb soda, and peony rose petals from the garden. Peonies are the only roses that I have growing in the garden, because I have the greatest affinity with them and, I know, I know. Germaine Greer would be all like, "Can women *please* start comparing themselves to something other than roses?" and I'd be all like, "Whatever, Germaine." Peonies are my homegirls.

I've got fluffy pink angel cheeks, voluminous fairy's petticoats, wholesome-looking etched salmons, electric yellow Claire de lunes, sumptuous coral charms, fuchsia-colored first arrivals, and wedding-gown-white mother's choices all moving in circles around one another, and they've gone absolutely wild. Their multiple layers delicately curl into themselves and flop outward with such abandon. I've hung a hammock next to where they're all planted so that I can emulate their state when I feel inspired to. Which is, like, every day.

I've also added a few drops of bergamot, sandalwood, and geranium essential oils to the bath because, together, they fill the space with a fragrance that smells like the chambers of ancient Egypt. Or at least what I imagine the chambers of ancient Egypt to smell like. It's how I'd hope for them to smell.

If there were one place I would like to travel to in three- and fourth-dimensional time and space it would be ancient Egypt. Which, of course, is problematic. And I don't really fly in planes, because I can't make sense of them. I can make sense of birds and insects, and the way that they fly, because people didn't make birds or insects, or come up with the way that they fly. I don't trust or understand the things that people make or come up with. I feel safer with nature. It's just there, for everyone to see, touch, taste, smell, and hear. There's a simplicity to it that puts me at ease.

Every season is like a teacher gently guiding me, and Christmas in Australia brings the greatest teaching of all: summer. Right now, it's Christmas Eve Eve, and it's the best. I've never had a white Christmas and I wouldn't want one. Every day since the beginning of December I've spent time lying on the glades outside, lapping up all of the negative ions, and feeling held and recharged. I've doused myself in DIY sunscreen—almond oil, coconut oil, zinc oxide, red raspberry seed, shea butter, and carrot seed—and life has made sense to my body, and my mind. The world and all of the strangeness of being here no longer seems baffling, or ridiculous. It seems obvious. I mean, of course I'm here, where else would I be?

Although, lying on the grass for too long can sometimes be disorienting: it starts to seep in that I have no beginning and no end, and that everything is moving and vibrating and I might fall into the sky. Then I remember that the earth and the sky are my real mother and father and lover, and I feel calm again.

5.

A few years ago I created an altar in a far corner of the garden because my shaman told me to. I picked a lingam stone from her mesa and she was all like, "That means you need an altar in your garden."

The one I've created is surrounded by pale-pink, plastic-looking wax flowers, and bright-red tree waratah, and it's filled with malachite and opals and diamonds, and special sticks and eucalyptus leaves, and different sizes of rosella and cockatoo feathers. There's hematite crystal and jasper spread in a circle around the whole thing, which is designed to shield and energize it in a totally peaceful and non-violent way. Then, at the center, there's a photo of my family, a watercolor drawing I did of Porkchop, and a signed poster of Heath Ledger. He's my guardian angel.

I once had a dream that he and I were walking around the garden together and he put his arm around me and said, "Here we are. Here we are. Here we are." Out of respect I always call him Heath Ledger. Not Heath, or Ledger, or Mr. Ledger, or Heathcliff, or something overly familiar and weird like that. I mean, I didn't know him personally, and I'm not a journalist who has to, like, shorthand things because it's the house style, or whatever.

So Heath Ledger's nearly illegible signature is sprawled across the center of a large poster of him as Ned Kelly, and the tagline of the poster reads, "You Can Kill a Man, But Not a Legend." It's sealed behind glass, and held by a frame, which is made of stone, and when I sit before it at a certain time of day, and gaze into its dark eyes in a certain kind of light, I can see my reflection.

I'm drawn to different parts of the altar depending upon my mood, and right now, I find the diamonds to be the most magnetizing part. I read somewhere that, once upon a time, the carbon found in diamonds was part of a living organism, which would mean that, technically, they're, like, alive. I've always thought that sparkling was a lot like laughing. So today I spent some quality time with the diamonds, before going through the process of caring for my physical being.

I like to get a sense of the weather before going out, and tonight, it's muggy and dense. There's a lot of pressure in the air. And smoke. Haziness has become a daily staple thanks to bushfires roaring outside the city. Large portions of the country are burning right now and grief is hanging in the air everywhere else. I bought a smoke mask and I haven't used it. No one seems to be using them, even though there's hardly any left in the shops. Australians don't like to be seen taking anything too seriously, mate.

Rain is definitely coming, though. We've had, like, three days of insistent sun, and smoky-blue skies, and relatively crisp mornings, which always leads to a storm.

It's the best weather for a party, though, because no matter how much everyone prepares, not one strand of hair is going to remain straightened, and not one armpit is going to be free of sweat. Thighs are going to stick to chairs, and shirts are going to cling to skin, and no one is going to be able to uphold their carefully constructed social facades, which is brilliant. May our collective fakery melt into the humidity and sink into the soil and evaporate into the air. Rest in peace, fakery. Not. Fakery will never rest. Not even in death.

It's also a full-blood-super-moon eclipse in Leo tonight. Once upon a time, lunar eclipses were seen as bad omens. People were told not to go outside during them because when the earth covers the moonlight it creates a sense of darkness devouring everything. So. I made sure to exfoliate really well and I'm just, like, hoping for the best.

I used a coffee-and-mint-leaf scrub to wake myself, and my skin, up. The power of being slathered in clumpy, crunchy mud cannot be underestimated. Well, the power of imagining one's self to be slathered in clumpy, crunchy mud cannot be underestimated. I'm pretty sure that you can buy beauty mud for this exact purpose, or that I could have literally gone outside and scooped some up with my hands. It's just that the coffee-

and-mint-leaf one I found came in this really sleek recycled-glass bottle, and, through buying it, I also purchased the idea of being a conscientious consumer, which felt pleasant.

Then I quickly showered in cold water to clear my auric field, and to get my metabolism and lymphatic systems going, and I left the windows of the bathroom open with the intention of inviting in an evening breeze. I ended up getting bitten by a mozzie on my thigh, shoulder, and pinkie finger. Now, I'm using every last ounce of discipline that I have in me not to scratch.

6.

About a week ago I put the Woolly Bush tree in the living room so that it could carry out its job as Resident Christmas Tree. My parents bought it the year that I was born, and it feels like a sibling. It's taller than me now, too. It's three meters high, and a native, and, technically, a shrub. So not exactly the most glamorous member of the Proteaceae family. However, it's a bronze-glowing Woolly Bush, which means that it has red tips on the ends of each branch. I've pruned it in a conical shape, and wound gold fairy lights around it, and positioned it in front of the enormous window that looks out over the front path. It's pretty regal. I keep the fairy lights going all of the time because I love to be able to see it gleaming at me whenever I walk down the path.

Underneath, there's a sea of gifts, which I've accumulated throughout the year. Porkchop has made a habit of exploring them, and falling asleep in between them, and clawing at their wrapping paper. Bits of red ribbon are now torn up and strewn all over the floor, and I'm not going to clean it up, because I enjoy living with a creature that has a relationship to things and that has made a conscious choice to tear up bits of ribbon and scatter them everywhere. It's his contribution to our Christmas cheer, and I would be a fool to clear it away for no real reason whatsoever.

At the top of the tree I've put an enormous, gold Magen David. I'm very into gold, and I'm very into stars, and I'm very into things that are of value to other people. I've also got a gold Chanukah menorah sitting on the windowsill in the kitchen, and, every night, I light the candles with the shamash before I cook. I treat the process of cooking and preparing and eating food as a sacred rite. My mum's mum always did this, too. Nana made the greasiest toasted cheese sandwiches, and poured the sweetest cups of tea, and her blintzes—when lightly seared on the pan and served with blueberries—were as sweet as they were sour, and her fruitcakes were as tart as they were heavy.

She was a full-bodied beauty and whenever we'd spend time together, we'd cook, eat, watch *The Nanny*, and play dress-ups with all of her clip-on earrings, and rings, and bracelets, and brooches, and watches, which were given to her by my grandfather and/or by an assortment of companions, admirers, and suitors, which she accumulated as steadily as she did accessories. Or she'd get me to paint her nails. Nana had a collection of pearly-colored polishes that were usually waiting for me on her bedside table along with cotton swabs and remover, in case I made a mistake as I took her hands into mine and decorated them.

Some of the polishes were a bit peach, or a bit pink, or a bit white, or a bit cream, and they all suited her. Everything about her was like mother of pearl. Her olive skin was cool to the touch, like seawater, and the iridescent tones of the nail polishes always matched her jewelry and accentuated her brown eyes and golden hair.

Her whole family was murdered during the Second World War. Well. *My* whole family was murdered during the Second World War. Sometimes I forget that, and I find myself thinking of them as her family, not mine. It's strange to think that we're all here because someone wasn't killed at some point.

A while ago I read somewhere that we're like mountains and that our day-to-day awareness is the front of who we are, where the sun shines, and everything we're afraid of is the back, in shadow, out of our awareness. Although, I have a strong feeling that my ancestors are at the back, and that there's nothing to be afraid of. Not really.

7.

I'll definitely paint my nails before leaving the house tonight, and I actually think that a pearly polish would go quite well with my outfit. I even have one called "Champagne Frost," which I suspect Nana would approve of, because my heart swells when I think about it. That's the best way to know anything, although no one ever tells you that. No one ever says, "Just use the expansive feeling in your chest to understand what's true, and what you want, and where to go, and what really matters," because they're too busy forcing you to learn from books that they're choosing, and pointing at whiteboards that they're writing on, and encouraging you to ask questions from curriculums that they've set.

Which is why I'm very proud to announce that all of the books in my possession are ones that I've chosen, and that have chosen me. They weren't recommended to me by anyone. No schoolteacher or university lecturer told me to write essays on their "core themes," and no bestseller list said that they were "ones to watch," and no girlfriend in a book group told me it changed her life. I've been drawn to each one, and they've been drawn to me.

Right now, Lisa Bellear's *Aboriginal Country* is beside my bed. She was an activist, artist, photographer, poet, comedian, playwright, broadcaster, and Goernpil woman of the Noonuccal people of Minjerribah. There's a street on the north side of Melbourne called Warrior Woman Lane, which is named after a line in one of her poems. It's actually more like an alleyway than a laneway, although that doesn't diminish its significance. Melbourne is filled with significant alleyways.

So before I fall asleep each night, Lisa Bellear tells me about the history of this land and her people. I want to do everything that I can to honor them, and their history, because unlike New Zealand, America, and Canada, Australia has no treaty with its Indigenous population. They weren't even legally recognized as citizens until 1967.

I always feel intimidated when I cross paths with them. I don't know how to build a bridge between who I am and who they are. Whenever I see an Aboriginal person I immediately feel out of place and ridiculous. It seems so absurd that I'm here. Surely I'm meant to be flouncing about somewhere tepid in the Northern Hemisphere, making daisy chains and milking cows.

It's confusing. I mean, if I don't know how to relate to Australia's Indigenous people, and I can't really make sense of why I'm here with them, I don't really know what being an Australian means. Like, if I can't fathom the link between who I am, and who they are, and why we're all here together, there must be something broken about the relationship that I have with who I am and where I'm from.

Which would make sense, because Australia is a broken country. Unresolved guilt, and trauma, and indebtedness to the Crown seem to define the very little history that we have. Aboriginal people possess a much longer, and much more intimate, relationship with this land. We were their apocalypse. They had been living on this continent for more than 60,000 years, and all of a sudden, and as of a minute ago, proportionally, we turned them into the most incarcerated people on the planet, and only just recently did we deem it inappropriate to, like, hunt them at random.

An American comedian once came here and did a tour and got into trouble for making jokes about how it was legal to hunt Indigenous Australians right up until the 1920s. I've always wondered if people were upset with him because he was joking about something so malevolent and fucked up, or because he was bringing up a subject that we're so deeply ashamed of. Maybe both.

I really want to be Australian; I just don't know how.

A few months ago, I watched a show about Aboriginal land rights and one of the elders from a community in Queensland stood up and said that the land owns us. All of us. Not the other way around.

So perhaps at the end of a stinking hot day, what makes me Australian is the fact that I took my first steps on its ground. My body is fueled by crops grown on its soil. My skin sweats in its humidity, and its waters hydrate and cleanse me. I wouldn't last two minutes without its air. I sleep under its stars every night, and I rub its aloe vera on my mozzie bites, and I coat my hair in masks made from its oils.

Because even if my hair cannot be tamed under any circumstances, the degree to which it's nourished can be—and my tresses feel like fucking satin now.

8.

Now the most empowering and revolutionary aspect of my pre-Christmas-Eve-Eve party ritual has arrived: the mirror. Hello, friend. I stand here, naked, before you. Sweaty, oily, fleshy, and fresh, looking into my own eyes, and noticing that the right one appears to be slightly smaller than the left. There are patches of skin on my chest, and around my knees, which are still red from my overly zealous scrubbing efforts. Out, damn spot! Oops, I am the spot. I look like an almanac.

The skin on my face is particularly dewy, because I'm ovulating. My forehead is shiny, and, from what I understand, foreheads aren't supposed to be shiny. They're supposed to stay in the dewy and/or matte arena, and, when they refuse to do so, all manner of products are meant to be harnessed and implemented so as to ensure that the horrors of an overly-shiny-forehead-situation are swiftly concealed and avoided, because an overly-shiny-forehead-situation exposes an unmanageable, sticky quality that is considered unbecoming in this day and age.

If our eyebrows are too bushy, or if our pores are too large, or if our under-eye bags are too noticeable, or if our teeth are too yellow, or too crooked, or if our wrinkles are too deep, or if our body parts are too large, or too soft, or too ripply, or vein-y, we're essentially supposed to go in for a day procedure before leaving the house. Or, at the very least, we're expected to become masters at hiding such unfortunate "humanities" behind all manner of makeup, clothing, falsely confident body language, hyaluronic acids, glycolic acids, virtual filters, collagen fillers, witty one-liners, blinding smiles, and carefully selected accessories, because these aren't seen as positive indicators of the fact of being alive, rather than dead.

Physical attributes such as shiny foreheads, and menstrual blood, and sweat, and sagging skin, and snot, and earwax, and belly button fluff, and cellulite, and dark body hair, and vaginal discharge, and phlegm, and facial lines, and scars are considered to be problematic and unsightly. They are not seen to be miraculous. Quite the contrary. In the eyes of society, the body's ability to heal and regulate itself is not cause for celebration. There really is no need for the hormones and fluids circulating through all 7.53 billion bodies on this planet to become public knowledge.

Certain physical attributes do carry power, however. For example, visible collarbones are revered, as are large, pert breasts, angular cheekbones, tiny waists, skin that is smooth, thighs with gaps between them, butt muscles that are tough and round, and lips that are full, and stomachs that are flat, and doe-eyes that are large.

Some days my features fit all of these categories, and on other days, they fit none of them at all. The way I relate to my body depends upon whatever else I am in the process of ignoring, or refusing to feel, or take action on, or give attention to. How it looks and feels is usually the by-product of something totally unrelated to it.

And I've noticed that people who focus very intently on their bodies are largely unfulfilled and listless. Their physical existence has become a trap, and they radiate a sense of boredom so potent that it has the capacity to make life seem futile for the rest of us.

It's as if after too much time looking in a mirror, or down a camera lens, they have nothing else to offer or believe in. Their life becomes a dead end, and every breath, step, tilt of hip, and pout whispers: "my body, my body, my body, help, help, help," and nothing more.

9.

Now my gaze is drawn to the tiny creases that sit between my upper arms and chest, which often distress me when I'm in changing rooms trying on singlets and strappy tops and boob tubes, because they seem so awkward and in the way. I mean, what's their function? Are they a part of my shoulder or my arm? Why can't they just move into my breast area?

I'm always inclined to push my breasts up with my hands when I'm naked in front of a mirror so as to reassure myself that if a more busty or buoyant quality were to be desired, it would be at my disposal. That is, if I were ever to wear a bra again. Which I wouldn't, because why would I.

The veins in my arms and hands and feet are protruding in the heat, and my pubic hair is damp and full. I haven't shaved my underarms or legs for a while, which is new for me. A guy I once dated found hairy legs and underarms to be dirty, and scuzzy, and whenever I'd toy with the idea of not shaving, he'd quickly swoop in and be all like, "Yeah, ok, well, why don't you go and buy some harem pants, and walk around the supermarket barefoot, and forage on the weekends, and be on welfare, and not wash your bed sheets, and chuck a crystal on, and take no responsibility, then?"

My belly looks quite flat from the side because I haven't eaten. I can never eat right before entering a social situation. Having to digest takes up too much energy. Earlier today I ate a bowl of pasta with extra-virgin olive oil and lemon juice, and fresh garlic and chili, and parsley from the garden, and salt and pepper, and nutritional yeast, which is going to see me through until I reach my post-party supper.

I always look forward to my post-party suppers. In a way, I look forward to them more than the parties themselves, and tonight is no exception. I've planned a lightly toasted salad sandwich, and my mouth is already watering. I mean, I don't want to end-game my experiences. Anything could happen tonight. I just like having something edible to look forward to.

One time I got home to a bowl of fresh strawberries, blackberries, blueberries, banana with cinnamon sprinkled on it, and crunchy, salty peanut butter, coconut yogurt, maple syrup, and linseed meal, and the guy I had wanted to spend time with all night finally contacted me and was like, "hey, soz we didn't get to hang—wink—can I still c u? wanna cum over to mine now? Xox."

I smelled the rose geranium essential oils burning at my bedside, and I looked down at my bowl of anti-oxidant-rich goodness, and I sensed the safety of my weighted blanket, and of my bed, and I glanced at the title of the book sitting next to me, *A Course in Miracles*, and I made eye contact with Porkchop, who was in the process of kneading in my lap, and I was like, yeah, um... no thanks.

My butt crease is sweaty. There are no patches of dry skin on my elbows or knees, which is good. My nana would be very happy about that. She was always whipping out large, round tubs of body lotion and slathering their contents on my extremities while shaking her head and chanting, "Never trust a woman with dry elbows! Never!"

Above the mirror, I have a large, blown-up portrait of Yazemeenah Rossi. It's from a shoot she did about makeup for women over the age of fifty. She's sixty-three, and the background is bright and white, and her hair is bright and white, and her smile is bright and white, and her eyes are deep, and round, and brown, with thick aqua eyeliner lacquered across the top of them. The old and the dead are the most rewarding people to idolize, because they know things that we don't.

Now I'll light a French candle and ritualize the act of loving and accepting myself, exactly as I am. Because I love and accept myself exactly as I am. I love and accept myself exactly as I am. I love and accept myself exactly as I am. I love and accept myself exactly as I am. I love and accept myself exactly as I am. I love and accept myself exactly as I am. I love and accept myself exactly as I am. I love and accept myself exactly as I am. I love and accept myself exactly as I am. I love and accept myself exactly as I am. I love and accept myself exactly as I am.

10.

I'm officially one step closer to leaving the sanctity of my sacred space in order to join my fellow human beings in the mortal realm. I'm playing with the idea of what to wear even though I already know, and I'm dancing for Porkchop, and drinking a martini, and putting on some of my nana's explosively floral perfume, because it enhances the feelings of nostalgia that I have about the fact of existing, and injects any nervousness I'm experiencing with a sense of destiny and inevitability. I have a funny feeling about tonight, and while I don't want to get my hopes up, I always do, because I'd rather get my hopes up than be down in the dark with doubt.

Earlier this evening I couldn't figure out how to connect the new speaker system, so I'm listening to a Spice Girls CD, and relishing in the sound of the first album I ever bought, while dressing up like the kid I was when I bought it. I loved wearing Mum's kimonos and dancing in the mirror when I was a child. It's like I knew I would be this person eventually and tonight she's so much fun. Oh my goddess, I can't think of anything better. It's the moment before the moment and I can breathe. Anything can happen from here, and I'm in love with myself.

I tried wearing red lipstick with the red kimono and it was overdoing things a bit, so I opted for a plum-like color called Wildwood. I like the name, there's poetry to it. *Wildwood.* It quells the nerves I have about being "too much," which are swiftly followed by the fears I have of "not being enough," before I reassure myself with things like the names of lipsticks, because I interpret them as signs that I'm on the right track and that everything is going to be ok.

Wildwood.

11.

I'm not sure what time it is. The one clock I have in the house is broken, and I prefer it that way. Fuck time. I feel uneasy around people who go by the time.

I once went out with a guy who never took off his watch. Checking it became this very stifling and very distinctive character trait. The weight of it made him seem more chained to the world, and to his idea of himself. It would just dangle there, heavily and ominously, as he'd sip a short black, and hold my face, and kiss my lips. Tick, tock, tick, tock.

One night he said that he had only stayed over to be "polite" because he actually had somewhere else to be at 10 a.m. the next day, and I felt very confused by this. I mean, was I supposed to say thank you? Why would he stay over when he'd prefer to leave? Or when he had somewhere *else* to be? "It would have been rude to go," he said. "It would've been *rude*."

Months later I ran into him and he said that he had to keep moving because he hadn't eaten, and it was lunchtime. Then he looked at his watch so as to be doubly sure that it was, in fact, lunchtime, before adding, "Yeah! It's two o'clock, see? It's lunchtime," as if Gregorian time was proof that, not only was it lunchtime, he was running late for it. The guy was running late for his own hunger. And he needed a socially sanctioned reason to leave my presence beyond the fact of simply wanting to.

I find it very hard to trust people whose wants and needs pale against the power of a clock, or the social pressures of being "polite." Nevertheless, I always, very politely, say good-bye to my paternal grandfather before I leave the house. If politeness has a place, it's definitely in our communications with the deceased. I have a watercolor self-portrait of him hanging over the front door. He watches over me even though I never met him. He was a property developer, and he spent a lot of time sketching birds, and flowers, and insects, and trees. So while property development existed on this large and imposing scale, what gave him pleasure remained small, intimate, and delicate.

I once found a sketchbook of his filled with tree trunks. His face in this particular self-portrait looks a bit like a tree trunk. It's different shades of brown and cream. It's long, and dense, and rough, and full of folds, and creases, and crevices, and pigmentation, and it dutifully watches over everyone who enters or exits the premises.

12.

I just got into a taxicab and requested that the radio be turned on as we roll into the possibilities of the night, and it's the best. I'm never too particular about which radio station needs to be turned on, although I'm always curious about what the driver will choose. It's part of the fun. In any case, there just needs to be music. Please give the moment that I've offered to myself a soundtrack: frame it with a melody, or I might want to turn around, and go back.

My driver tonight didn't ask me what music I wanted to listen to. He went straight to the classical music station before saying that he "hates" this country, because the seasons never change. I think hearing a few bars of Vivaldi's *Four Seasons* performed by the Budapest Strings Chamber Orchestra tipped him over the edge. "It always the same," he kept repeating. "Always . . . the same."

Nothing seems the same to me. Ever. I won't say anything, though. I'll just smile, because sometimes it's best to say nothing and to smile when you're stuck in a situation with someone who is having a diametrically opposed experience of it. Especially when they're, like, driving you at 40 mph in a four-thousand-pound piece of machinery.

The first time I learned about the power of not saying things was when I was staying in the Victorian goldfields with a boyfriend. We were in this shack on someone's farm, and one night, I went outside to look at the stars, and he came out, and he had his eyes cast to the ground, and was kicking a brick, and feeling frustrated, and complaining about his cough, and wishing that we were somewhere else, because he felt isolated and jaded, and he wanted to go back to the city. While he was talking, I looked up and saw a shooting star. I laughed, and he asked why, and I said that it was funny how two people could be having such different experiences, simultaneously, and he went, "I don't want to go into that right now."

13.

We're driving through the city and I'm looking out the backseat window and thinking of the opening sequence of an American film that's seen through a backseat window. Most of Melbourne's streets are deserted, because everyone is making the most of the department stores being open after hours. Tomorrow night, on Christmas Eve, they're going to be open around the clock. 'Tis the season of overspending and overextending, and if people aren't busy shopping, they're attending office Christmas parties, and napping after seafood lunches, and smiling too much, and wearing too little, and getting sunburned on rooftops, and balconies, and giving gifts that nobody needs, and watching children tire of playing with new toys within the confines of overly manicured backyards.

Or they've started their drives to the beach, or they're flying overseas to visit Aunt Ida in England, or Holland, or wherever, and the rest of the city has fallen quiet in the heat. It's just whoever's left, and the steaming streets. All of the buildings, and the native and imported plants, finally have room to breathe and to rest.

Getting lost in Melbourne at this time of year is such a blessing. The common jasmine vines are singing sweet, sensual songs over every fence, and down every laneway, and the boronias are bursting. Mum once told me that even the roses turn up their scent after sunset in the summer, and it's true. They do. I recently watched a documentary that said relishing in the scent of a flower—any flower—is essentially relishing in the scent of a sex organ. How hot is that.

Exotic trees and flowers and bushes line Melbourne's streets. The lavender and the daisies and the jacarandas and the camellias take on an almost supernatural quality, because they're slightly larger, slightly brighter, and slightly stronger than the ones you'll see in other parts of the world. The climate and the soil here have forced them to become the hardiest version of themselves. They've been pressed against the harshness of the red dirt, and orange dust, and dull greens, and small leaves, and silvery grays of native saltbushes, and wattles, and eucalyptus trees, which can be so ruthless and muscly.

The soil is often complex, dry, and heavy. Working it out and working with it is not for the impatient or faint of heart. Colonized Australia is a very young country, and creating a melodious, fertile, multicultural environment, which can endure its unforgiving conditions, requires time and effort.

I've managed to coordinate the garden in such a way so as to make the most of what Melbourne's summertime has to offer, and it accommodates for all kinds of flora and fauna. I've carefully arranged the gardenias, hibiscus, and jasmine so that they line the walkways, and native wisteria weeps from each archway. I like coming home and strolling around—especially at dusk—because it's such a symphony of smells.

Except the mosquitoes have a party around the same time each night, too. They flit about among the hare's-foot ferns and ponds and fountains. Yeah. Don't let those Nymphaea "Helvola" waterlilies bearing extraordinary blooms seduce you into believing that protection isn't necessary. Dousing in lavender oil at dusk is a must. Although, I read somewhere that being bitten by bugs represents guilt in our systems that needs purging. So, technically, the bugs are doing us a favor when they bite us.

Around the garden there's heaps of light and shade and a few gentle wind tunnels. I've introduced soil that's rich with nitrogen, potassium, and phosphorus, although not too much. The natives aren't as keen on phosphorus as the exotics are. Everyone has dietary requirements, which are important to be mindful of if we want to be able to live harmoniously together.

I've had a very efficient and very intricate bore-watering system installed, and I fertilize when you're supposed to, and I pull weeds, because isn't it fabulous and satisfying to do that. I have a super-juicy compost bin filled with leftovers, and the gardener once told me that dried leaves make for great mulch, so I often gather them up and sprinkle them on different flower beds. Even the dead are useful.

I talk to most of the plants every day, and I don't discriminate between the natives and the exotics. All of the interactions that

I have are stimulating. I always learn something, and there's always something to be learned. The crowded perennial beds are very chatty, and they absolutely thrive alongside the golden wattles—which smell like semen for some reason?—and the incense plants—which smell like bananas at a certain time of the morning? When differences are appreciated, and cared for, any conversation can be had.

Droughts always put the exotics in their place, though. They're a reminder of the stubbornness and wherewithal of the natives, which evolved within the Australian landscape. The exotics didn't, and they struggle to survive unless they work some shit out, and grow deeper roots and thicker thorns.

14.

The moonlight is piercing its way through a dense layer of cloud and it looks close, low, and yellow. I usually ask the cabdriver to stop a block or so away from the location I'm going to, because I like to give it an opportunity to call out to me. I like to sense it writhing from a distance. It doesn't take a dog to sniff out a good party. Usually, you can just follow the sound of laughter, and of people not listening to each other, and of a reverberating, hypnotic bass. And if you can't sense these things from the street, then you're probably not going to the party that you thought you were.

I once had a conversation with my dad about electronic music, and hypnotic basses, and why I love them so much, and he didn't get it at all. I mean, who can blame a guy who was raised by Roy Orbison, Elvis Presley, and The Four Seasons? We learned completely different musical languages as children.

In order for him to appreciate what electronic music and a repetitive bass can mean to a person and that, yes, they are real, and meaningful, because they vibrate, like everything else in the universe, I had to explain that it feels like a heartbeat.

And the fact that a synthesizer is used, and words often aren't, doesn't make electronic music any less considered, experiential, or original. I say my prayers in electro every day. I like anything that makes the act of breathing, or walking down a street, or even just thinking, seem epic—and I don't like words being put in my mouth.

I resent lyricists for speaking at me. Unlike Dad, and many of the people that I've been in intimate relationships with, I don't appreciate having every little thought and feeling told to me in a story, and explained and repeated and harmonized between different rhythms and beats, and put into different sequences, and told to me over and over again.

I've tried to cultivate a greater appreciation for this. It's just that one boyfriend refused to play the music of certain musicians that he admired in my presence, because he felt "weird" about it. I'm all for sacred space, and I would never have wanted to intrude upon his special time with these artists, or with their music. It's just that when I wanted to explore their work, and what it might mean to me, he said that this made him feel "uncomfortable."

His possessiveness in this regard said a lot about the relationship that he must have had to his thoughts, and to his feelings, because if these musicians were giving a voice to them, and he didn't want to share that voice with me... Then I guess he didn't want to share anything with anyone at all. He wanted to experience himself, alone, in a room, with the voices of people that he didn't know, and who didn't really care about him.

15.

I've traveled on foot for a few blocks now, and there are dense vibrations radiating from an enormous terrace house. It's almighty, dilapidated, and gray. It looks like the Addams Family's home on Cemetery Lane. It's decorated with hundreds of fairy lights, which look like illuminated cobwebs. They're electric blue, yellow, green, and red. There's silver tinsel winding its way up some tree trunks, and invading most of the bushes and shrubs. A crooked, white-picket fence has red baubles dangling from it.

There's definitely some black magic swirling around. The best parties often have a bit of black magic swirling around them. It's like homeopathy: we need to ingest a bit of the poison in order to heal and become stronger. I often use justifications like this for going to parties because if I didn't, I'm not sure why I would go to them at all.

The best party I've ever been to was in a mansion more modern than this one, and the family that lived in it was in the process of moving out. I think the girl who threw the party's dad was in publishing, and his second wife was a second wife, and they were moving to a loft in New York or something. He had thick-rimmed glasses, and gray hair sprouting out of a turtleneck, and second wifey was in designer velour tracksuits, holding chilled glasses of sav blanc, and smiling regardless of what was happening or being said.

Their home had glass doors and polished marble floors, and at the time of the party the furnishings were covered in plastic, which was just as well. The party was messy. The theme was "derelict," and everything about that night was politically incorrect. I still recall fragments of pseudo-intellectual conversations that I had with people in bathtubs, and of moments making out with mirrors, and of watching flowers falling from suit jacket pockets.

Just before dawn, a guy who identified himself as A Male Model—as if to reassure others that he wasn't letting his beauty be neglected, that he was putting it to good use—who had caramel hair and skin and eyes, and who spoke with his hands, kissed me into cunnilingus on the steps of the swimming pool. He didn't seem to care about breathing or about introductions. He came home with me and we made love after the sun was up, before I cooked scrambled tofu for breakfast, and we never saw each other again.

16.

Apparently, the French aristocracy used to dress up as the homeless and throw epic balls. Although, if you had asked anyone about this at the derelict party, I doubt they would've known. Most of the attendees were very privileged people, and very privileged people don't generally take the time or put in the effort to honor the origins of things.

Far too often, privilege seems to be the result of conquering things, and stealing things, and copying things, and trying to make money out of things, before moving on to the next thing to conquer, steal, copy, and make money out of.

Australia is supposed to be one of the most privileged countries in the world, and we eat our national emblems for tea, and kill koalas while we're driving, and knock down heritage-listed buildings in order to erect apartment blocks, and destroy the Great Barrier Reef in the name of constructing coal mines, and our unemployment benefit hasn't been raised in twenty-five years, and we invite tourists to trample all over Uluru-Kata Tjuta National Park, and yet we refuse to offer asylum to refugees.

It's as if nothing is sacred to us except for money and our own whiteness. We don't care for what we have. We don't use our so-called privilege very responsibly so, more often than not, we don't seem very privileged at all.

All I have to offer Australian soil is the sound of my high heels slamming against the pavement as I approach this behemoth of a building. And what a rhythmic and foreboding air their sound creates. We can probably thank some overweight, middle-aged man like Alfred Hitchcock or Pedro Almodóvar for making sure that something so damaging to a woman's body has become synonymous with her mystery and power.

Oh, dear. My heart always starts racing as I approach the future audience to the fact of my existence. Tonight I'm channeling my Atlantean Breast Plate, which is adorned with emeralds, garnet, pearl, peridot, and lapis lazuli. When I'm menstruating, it includes moonstone.

I'm imagining its soft, rose-gold aura, all around my body, sparkling, and deflecting negative energy, and transmuting it into something good for the earth and all of its inhabitants to reduce, reuse, and recycle.

The gate has opened with a screech. I can't close it properly, so I'm going to leave it open. I'm moving along a tea-candle-lit path, and a rather unromantic and incongruent sensor light has blinded me, and I can see a handwritten note on the front door that reads, “walk around the side / no throwing cigarette butts over the fence like last time / merry xmas biatches / we’re watching,” and I don’t do as I’m told.

I’m yours, party. Take me away.

17.

I'm standing outside and so far I have nothing to say to anyone, and I like it that way because it makes me seem more interesting. It's amazing what not speaking can do for other people in terms of levels of interest.

I'm leaning against a fence and feeling grateful for the fact that I brought vodka and a martini glass and olives and toothpicks with me, because I want to enjoy myself, and I know what I like. I'm not going to drink beer, and skull fermented grapes and the remnants of milk and eggs from some random's goon bag, in order to fit in and behave like a non-threatening prop in the mise-en-scène of someone else's night.

People at parties are always "doing" drugs and I never feel like "doing" them. A friend once told me that I already live in a fantasy, so I have no need to "do" drugs. The experience that I already have of the world is so psychedelic and sensual.

I also don't like having to thank someone or something outside of myself for what I experienced the night before. I want my life, and everything inside of it, to be absolutely mine. I don't want to be indebted to a laboratory, or to a plant, or to a guru, or to a doctor, or to some guy who cooks in his basement. I want to give myself to myself, fully.

One time I went to a doctor about some paperwork that I needed for something completely unrelated to anything medical, and she asked me if I was taking prescription medication. Like, was I on anti-anxiety meds or anti-depressants, perhaps? I tried to explain to her that I didn't feel comfortable having my feelings meddled with. She looked at me over her teeny-tiny glasses and insisted that taking medication might help me "deal with difficult feelings" and I said no thank you before sharing with her that feelings weren't supposed to be "dealt" with, they were supposed to be "felt" with.

She remained silent, and I took that silence as an opportunity to go on to say that no matter how hard it might be to feel feelings, and to think thoughts, they're all that I have, and they mean a lot to me. She craned her neck like she wanted to get a look down my throat for some reason, and I looked up at her and said, "Meditation not medication," and she clicked the end of a pen with a company logo on it, cocked her head to one side, and replied, "Well, if you ever change your mind."

Which I won't, because my mind is the most powerful weapon that I have, and I'm not about to fuck with it via the use of drugs that I could never fully understand the implications of, nor am I about to "change" my mind for a doctor who feels at ease making money out of people's vulnerability.

I mean, Traditional Chinese Medicine doctors make money when their patients are healthy not when they're scared and sick. So. Sorry, Doctor. If anyone's "mind" needs "changing," it's yours.

18.

There's a girl who keeps looking at me standing here, and she's smiling as she speaks to someone else. It occurs to me that my sexuality is more fluid in my mind than it is in 3D. I often wish that my sexual desires were more malleable than they are. Being solely attracted to men sucks. It's like suffering from an irreversible case of Stockholm syndrome. I'm drawn to the very creature that has violated, oppressed, exploited, raped, kidnapped, subjugated, controlled, made fun of, manipulated, abused, belittled, objectified, persecuted, and condescended me and my people for centuries.

Even my fantasies about women involve men. I have purely woman-centric fantasies closer to my period, because I think it's like making love to myself, and to the body that I've been given, during a particularly psychic and exposing window of time. I'm also a bit obsessed with big breasts because I suspect that I wasn't breastfed for long enough, and that my food-refusing tendencies during adolescence got in the way of adequate nurturing, and nourishment. So, yeah. Big breasts represent the ultimate in womanly lusciousness, and sustenance, and it's very easy for me to fantasize about them.

When I was touching myself recently, and dreaming away, I looked down and for the first time was aroused by my own tits. I sensed the weight of them against the bedspread and it unearthed a level of comfort and sensuality that I hadn't accessed before. Then I orgasmed, and wept, and laughed, and I felt really happy to be alive for a minute.

I don't think that this girl is sexually attracted to me, or that she has especially large breasts. She certainly wants something, though. She's cute and blond and manipulative, which can be very endearing in the right lighting. Just about anything can be endearing in the right lighting. Even being murderous. I mean. *Somebody* fell for it.

She's wearing a wide-brimmed, deep-purple felt hat, with a feather in it, and a big dark wrap around her shoulders, with soft black jeans, and little black sneakers poking out the bottom. She must be very hot, temperature-wise. And she doesn't appear to have a bag, or to be wearing makeup. Nevertheless, the whole shebang seems self-conscious and labored. She wants to seem sure of herself, and she's not. While the outfit and the lack of makeup appear to be making a statement of simplicity and ease, she's getting no pleasure out of it. Her body language is so constricted and tense. Her elbows are locked against her torso, and her jaw is tight, and her eyes are squinty, and every movement she makes is speedy, and small, and calculated. Although she desperately wants to be seen, she doesn't want to take up space. She doesn't know who she is. She can barely concentrate on the people in front of her, because she's so overcome with a desire to take who they are from them.

Demons and all of the scary creatures that we read about in stories are real. They aren't made up. Just look around. There are trolls on construction sites, and witches behind cash registers, and zombies parading en masse down city streets. I once read about a phenomenon called "Psychological Gargoyling," which is, like, a clinical term for when children take on the "evil" traits of their parents in order to survive the trying circumstances that they were brought up in. So, yeah. The monster isn't under your bed. It's your mum.

This girlwoman is like a vampire wanting a quick bite of everyone in order to stay alive. She's fueling herself from a source outside of herself. She can't stand to be alone with her own thoughts, or feelings. Not even for a second. Her conscious mind—and all of the choices stemming from it—completely revolve around seeking sustenance from others, and, right now, she's hungry. Starving, even.

"Good lord, girl. That kimono. Amazing!"

"Thank you."

"Where did you get it?"

"I don't really want to answer that, if that's ok."

"Oh, ok? Why not?"

"Because...I'm not my kimono."

"Um. What do you mean?"

"I'm not my kimono."

"Of course you're not. I was just...trying to make conversation?"

"Sorry. I guess I'm not very good at that kind of conversation."

"Whatever. I still like your kimono! Merry Christmas."

Ok, so that was death before dying and not in a good way. She has literally walked off and not looked back. Sometimes every attempt I make to connect and to communicate in a different way seems futile, and I fear that change is impossible, and that persecution is inevitable for us all.

I feel bad for not playing by the rules of the style of conversation that she feels at ease with, and that most people would facilitate for her. She probably perceives herself as being misunderstood and rejected, just like I do. Goddammit. I want to run after her and explain my workings out. Socially, that would seem insane: me, powering across party lines, kimono flying, Madame Butterfly-and-we're-off-to-the-opera, high heels smashing into the concrete, hand touching her shoulder, face turning, eye contact for the first time, before speaking, and saying something, something powerful, something uniting, something else.

She was so focused on my garments, and on my physique, that she could barely look me squarely in the face. Often when I meet a woman for the first time I want to shout, "I'm up here! I'm up here!" while pointing at my eyes, and smashing at my chest.

A friend once told me that when another woman compliments our clothes or our appearance, it's not about the clothes or our appearance. It's about the fact that socially, and culturally, we seem to be standing out, or fitting in. We're "winning" in terms of what's expected of us, and we're being admired for that. Then everyone wants to know how we're "doing" it and where we "got it." Which, unfortunately, doesn't make communicating or connecting any easier. In fact, it makes it impossible.

There's nothing to say when who and what we are is reduced to something that can be readily bought at a local vintage market or department store. There's nothing to learn or to discover. We become the sum total of a steady stream of receipts, not revelations. We can just buy each other off the shelf. Yep, one kimono, one pair of high heels, some spandex, a mulberry lipstick, a bottle of body oil, a martini, maybe a few sessions at the gym. Easy. Answering her question would have been the equivalent of saying, "Why, yes. Of course you can purchase/be me."

The problem is that we're not our things and we aren't just things. We didn't all die, and now the only way to learn about one another is to go through the belongings that we left behind. We aren't demographics, statistics, trends, or the outcomes of last season's stocktake sale.

Nevertheless, we've reduced ourselves to that. We've given our power over to the material world because it seems more quantifiable and manageable. Our conversations start there, and our conclusions about the world end there. The infinite, miraculous, mysterious nature of who and what we are has become a bit tedious.

So short, clear answers, directions, steps, and plans—with fixed outcomes—are appreciated, thank you very much. Let's chat about the location where we all "found ourselves" as distinct from what we found or the process of finding it.

It's far easier to reel off lists of shops, and retreats, and job titles than it is to engage with the process of self-discovery, which isn't always easy to articulate and, sorry, it's just that we don't really have the time to wait around for every little thought and feeling to be considered, expressed, and shared. There are more important things to be done and bought and planned for, and more important people waiting around who are more ready, willing, and able to be reduced to the confines of their stuff, and things, and shit.

Maybe it'd be easier if we were all chairs. I mean, a chair has a specific design, and a brand, and a price tag, and it sits wherever we put it down, and it stays there, and we can find comfort in it for as long as we want to rest our arses on it, and then we can move on from it, and it won't take offense to that, and it'll still be there when we return, no questions asked.

What a perfect companion.

19.

I'm not sure what to do with myself now. No physical gesture or action I want to take seems socially appropriate. Well, hardly anything I ever want to do seems socially appropriate.

In the parallel universe where I'd rather be, I'm taking off these ridiculous restrictive shoes, and stomping on the ground with my bare feet, and doing the best version of a haka that I could muster because, obviously, I'd be doing a haka without knowing anything about a haka. I'd simply be calling what I was doing a haka, because what I often do in the garden when I'm feeling exasperated is stomp my feet, and punch the air like it's alive, and jump up and down, and shake, and poke my tongue out, and open my eyes wide, and growl, and claw at the soil, and smack at the earth until I'm panting and exhausted, and I fall asleep right there on the ground.

I guess I'll just stand here with my empty martini glass, like a statue. I can sense strands of hair hanging against my cheeks, and the lipstick on my lips has become dry, and developed a musky taste. I'm a dusty cupboard filled with old clothes, and shoes, and decades-old makeup. My lower back has started to ache, or maybe it's been aching for a while? I just took a big belly breath and a vertebra behind my heart cracked.

There are fairy lights draped across the balcony, and people talking and smoking, and, from a distance, everyone looks like they're dressed in black, or navy, even though they aren't. They've been swallowed by the night. I can hear hip-hop and I can't discern the words, even though I know that it's hip-hop. Or trap. Or something.

I wish I had more woman friends and that I could more easily make woman friends. If I were to have a wedding right now, I have no idea who would be the maid of honor. If I were to have children right now, I have no idea who would be their godmother. I think I'm a seasonal companion. People try me on when the temperature is right. Wearing me too early or too late in the season doesn't feel natural. So it's best to just put me back in the closet until the right weather comes around, and I'm useful again.

The cement beneath my high heels is merciless. I'm leaning on a thick glass table with a tad too much of my weight. It's just that I don't want to sit down on one of the three chairs that are here, because that would suggest a level of commitment to this particular spot that I don't have, and I don't want to become trapped at this location by someone who misinterprets my sitting down as an invitation, or as an opportunity to distract themselves from themselves, because they're just as lost and disillusioned as I am, yet too scared to stand anywhere on their own and just be with themselves for a minute. Plus, I want to be able to move on from this location when I want to move on from it without having to navigate niceties.

Oh, no. There's my ex-boyfriend. He looks so strung out. Not skinny or anything. Just gray. He must be doing a lot of drugs. I've never seen him in sandals with socks before. Nor have I ever seen him without a beard. He's smoking rollies, too. Geez. I don't mind the bucket hat. Although, what's with the tote bag? What possessions does he have to carry? He must think that it makes him look artistic, progressive, laissez-faire, and inspired, or whatever. Because he certainly isn't artistic, progressive, laissez-faire, and inspired, or whatever. He's a very materialistic and very conservative kind of guy.

When we were together he was in the midst of a very corporate and very cashmere phase. He was working at his dad's company, and driving his mum's spare 4WD, and snowboarding at Mount Buller on the weekends, and competing with his brother, and with his mates, and basically with everyone, all of the time.

Even the sex that we had was competitive. He got off on the locations that we "fucked" in, and on the price of the sheets, and on what important person might walk in on us, and on what he could "do" or have "done" to him. The quality of the connection that we had, or how our bodies felt, didn't matter so much. It was about what "moves" we could "make" on each other, and whether or not he'd be able to "cum" and then smoke a dart, and drink a glass of champagne, and tell someone he wanted to impress about it. He was more interested in crafting an image of himself than actually being himself. It took up all of his time and energy, and, in the end, it bored me.

Although, the feeling of being pitted against everyone and everything in his life still haunts me. It stripped me of a piece of my humanity, and, ever since, I've been tentatively trying to reclaim it. I really don't want to talk to him right now. He reminds me of a part of myself that I'm still angry about losing. Probably because I didn't lose it, I gave it away.

One time we were at a dinner party with his friends and, between courses, he asked me to make some of the noises that I made during sex, and when I refused to do so, he imitated them, and everybody laughed.

"Hey!"

"Hey."

"I thought it was you."

"Hmm."

"How are you?"

"Good."

"Have you met Rain?"

"Rain?"

"My new girlfriend."

"Oh, no. Not yet."

"She'll be around somewhere. She's amazing."

"I bet."

"Different from you, though."

"I... would assume."

"Yeah."

"Do you live together?"

"We rent a room in Northcote. It's huge, and it has a balcony. Rain has planted all of these little flowers and herbs in these massive pots. You'd like it, I think. And Rain is super-chill. She's a naturopath and a photographer. She also models. Used to model, sorry. You'd get on really well, I think. Or maybe you'd clash? I dunno."

"Cool."

"You seeing anyone?"

"Umm... No."

"Really?"

"I wouldn't lie."

"No? Not to protect my feelings?"

"I . . . don't think so."

"You're hilarious."

"Hmm."

"Do you know anyone here?"

"No, I don't think so."

"You don't mind that, though, do you? You've always loved a party full of randoms."

"I guess."

"I still can't do that."

"What?"

"Rock up somewhere I don't know anyone."

"Right."

"You're looking really good."

"Yeah?"

"Yeah."

"What does 'good' mean?"

"I dunno. Fit?"

"Ah."

"Maybe let's find Rain. She must be around."

"It's ok, I don't want to force it."

"Are you nervous?"

"About . . . meeting her?"

"Yeah."

"Ah. No."

"Lol! You haven't changed."

"Ok?"

"What?"

"Nothing?"

"What?"

"It's ok."

"Well. There's someone I need to go and say hey to. We cool? What're you doing for Christmas? The usual?"

"Yeah. The usual."

"Ok, well. Have a merry one."

I don't know why people try to be friends with their exes. I mean, we were never friends, so why try after having decided that an intimate relationship isn't going to work? Friendships are intimate, too. You can't just, like, turn the connection down a notch and hope to make it better. It's still the same connection, and if it's faulty it's going to stay faulty.

I have no idea how I lasted eleven months with that guy. It's hard to fathom all of the brunches, and mornings in bed, and awkward dinners with his brother, and with his parents, and friends, and all of the hours spent watching violent films, and driving to the beach and back, and to the snow and back.

Even during the space of a five-minute conversation, he couldn't resist directly and indirectly comparing me to another woman at least three times, as if we were different models of car, or vacuum cleaners with slightly different functions.

He's certainly taught me a lot about how shitty people use competition and constant comparison as a distraction so as to not have to take responsibility for their shitty worldview.

When we were together, he would often go to the extent of trying to create competition and comparison between others so that his own shortcomings went unnoticed.

Whenever I'd call him out on how he related to women and I'd say something like, "Hey, I think you might be objectifying/infantilizing her a bit," or "Hey, maybe get a bit less touchy feely with people you don't know very well, because it seems a bit invasive," or "Hey, I think the way that you were staring at her might have made her uncomfortable," his reply would be, "Oh, you're just jealous that I'm talking to her," or "Oh, you're threatened by her, aren't you?" or "She's like one of the guys, ok? Some chicks are like that," or "She's just super at home with her sexuality. You could probably learn a thing or two from that."

Even talking about other women, and observing their behaviors, and analyzing their choices, was always interpreted as an attempt to impress him, and to make myself seem more superior. It wasn't deemed to be a mechanism for better understanding myself or others. It wasn't indicative of a desire to learn, or to grow, or to, you know. Think. He assumed everything I did was a way of trying to get his attention and approval. He couldn't comprehend that what I felt, and what I thought, wasn't always about him, or happening in relation to him.

It's true that some people put other people down in order to make themselves appear more desirable. They'll, like, talk themselves up, and act in a way that they think highlights their strengths, and magnifies others' weaknesses. Women are especially good at this. We're experts at manipulating and maneuvering other people's perceptions of us because, once upon a time, our survival depended upon it. Knowing how to push a man's buttons, and how to shape his reality, was a matter of life or death. However, in the case of the relationship that I had with this guy, survival was dependent upon my leaving him. Not upon my impressing or manipulating him.

I feel sorry for Rain. Because it really doesn't matter how beautiful, sensitive, talented, or intelligent you are: being treated like an object can destroy you.

20.

I'm finding it hard to breathe. I suffer from this condition where I really hope that socializing is going to go well, and when it doesn't, I feel helpless, and I don't know what to do with myself, and I start spinning. I've fainted before, too. Like, in this same situation. I've totally blacked out. I read somewhere that falling into a coma is a way to escape from someone that you don't want to have to deal with.

I used to negate difficult feelings by trying to tell myself that "nothing much" had happened during what I had actually experienced to be a distinctly unpleasant and/or disorienting encounter. I'd delude myself into thinking that it literally hadn't happened. I'd be like, "it was nothing, don't worry about it" or "whatever" or "I'll just quickly forgive them!" or "it's fine!" or "it's their responsibility, not mine," or "it doesn't bother me" or "it's all good don't worry about it" or "sorry, my bad!" or "it's cool, so what?"

I couldn't be fine with shit not being fine. That is, until I learned that the ancient Egyptians didn't believe in the concept of "zero" or "nothingness." They saw it as poison. Even nothing is something.

Energies and emotions affect physical reality just like sound, and gravity, and electricity, and music, and oxygen do. They breathe, and expand, and throb, and rush, even if we cannot name or understand them. It doesn't matter where we're from, or what we believe, or what language we speak. Millions of us are feeling the exact same way, right now, and we are united because of it.

21.

Maybe I'll go for a walk around the block and get some air. I like to go for little walks while I'm at parties. It gives me a chance to come into contact with myself again, and nobody notices. Besides. I'm already walking nowhere in particular right now so I may as well just . . . walk out the front gate. I don't know. I'm constantly feeling a need to "go outside" and "get some air" even though I'm already outside, breathing the air.

Oh, I just saw this girl I've occasionally had brunch dates with. She's one of those people who I think I'm supposed to get along with. Like, there's an affinity between us on some level. I've often felt obliged to make time for her, yet she's always spent our brunch dates describing the people that she's dating or crushing on as being "small" and "unsure" and "needy," and generally coming to the conclusion that the downfall of almost all of these relationships has been due to the fact that the other person was "small" and "unsure" and "needy" and that she doesn't "do" "smallness" and "uncertainty" and "neediness."

She calls herself a leader, and a teacher, and a speaker, and a content creator, and she shares images of herself in bikinis doing yoga poses on different beaches with captions telling everybody to "look deeper" and to "go within," and I've always felt a bit unnerved by not knowing who is taking the pictures.

The act of being photographed often looks like it happens by itself, or by chance, even though it doesn't. I once read a story about this thirteen-year-old model in Brazil who said that more than thirty people were involved in curating every single image ever taken of her, even when it looked as though she was alone and super-casual and taking it of herself.

Anyway. This girl also sees herself a writer, although for some reason she frequently quotes other writers, and playwrights. I've never really known why she, or why anyone, would do that. Especially when we have an entire universe of thoughts and feelings and languages and words at our disposal. Using someone else's seems a bit lazy and a bit inaccurate. The world needs new experiences and thoughts and feelings, and new ways of expressing them.

Sometimes, when she quotes herself, she writes her name at the bottom, I think in an attempt to copyright what she's said. She even puts little quotation marks around it, and chooses a special font, and a pastel-colored background. Maybe she does this as a way to stand out, or to stop others from plagiarizing her work? Actually. It must be a way to encourage others to quote her quotes. Yeah. Kind of like a salesperson, or a marketing pitch. Like, through presenting her words in this way, they look like they were written or spoken by a famous and important person. She definitely wants to be seen as a famous and important person. Not a needy, small, uncertain person.

The only problem is that truly famous and important people don't put their names at the end of sentences that they've written. Like, other people do that. Shakespeare didn't go, "to be or not to be" and then put a dash and his name after it in capital letters with a funky pattern and a pastel-colored background.

The line "to be or not to be" was created in a very certain context, in the throes of a very certain reality, and it came from the mouth of a very certain, and very complex, character, who was both an extension of Shakespeare and, equally, not Shakespeare. It was Hamlet, Prince of Denmark. So. To put Shakespeare's name immediately after "to be or not to be" is factually incorrect.

"Babe!"

"Hello."

"You'll never guess what just happened."

"I might?"

"Really?"

"I won't, though. You seem eager to tell me."

"I am!"

"What happened?"

"He's here. Yep. Over there. Can you see? Lol! Don't look! You're hilarious. Is he looking? Actually, don't worry about it. Have I filled you in? Well. After everything that happened the other week, he and I didn't speak, or have contact, and he just turns up here. Like... Fuck. Me. It's weird because when I was getting dressed tonight I had a feeling he was going to be here. I was over there just talking with this other guy, like, completely innocently, and he comes up clearly wanting to be included in the conversation. Like, what the fuck, right? After everything! It was so off-putting to the dude I was talking to. He was cute, too. He works as a bartender at that place that just opened. Well, it opened a year ago. It was in the paper. Anyway. I didn't know how to introduce them, so the other guy offered to go and get me another drink to, like, make shit less awkward, and he never came back. I don't blame him. I wouldn't mind that beer now, though. Ha-ha. Oh, well. Your skin looks fantastic ATM, BTW. Are you still into all of that amazing probiotic and prebiotic shit? And going to the gym and whatever? I was trying these green smoothies for a while and being really diligent about it and having them every morning and soaking the oats and refrigerating the flaxseeds and blending the celery, doing all of the things and after a while I just stopped for some reason and I'm not sure why. Anyway. Where was I? Oh shit, he's totally looking! Did you see that? I fucking felt it before I saw it! We're so connected. It's killing me. Is my hat ok? Is it better when the feather is on the side, or at the front? Or maybe at the back? I haven't tried the back. Did you see that other fucking girl with the felt hat and the feather? What a mung bean. I've been wearing felt hats with feathers for, like, months, and she's totally seen me out, and now here she is, wearing the hat, thinking that she owns that look or whatever. Anyway. So. He and I left things the other week at like, 'Let's cool off and think about what we both want,' and he didn't contact me after that. We hit the classic point where the guy gets scared, because he starts to question what it all means. Like, what does she expect? What do I do? I better start airing so that I don't have to take responsibility. You move an inch past being a guy's fuck buddy and he flips his shit. Merely raising the fact that we might need space to think about what we both wanted was probably what psyched him out. At the time he seemed chill about it. It was just when I was reflecting on the whole thing during that luxurious week I had without any fucking contact that I realized he had most definitely freaked out and most likely ditched. And tonight he was all like 'Hey, how are you' and I'm like ah . . . are you on crack, mate? He actually had the audacity to act like everything was normal and, like, chill, or whatever, and I'm like, wah?! So I go, 'I'm fine . . . How are you?' And played it really cool. Except that he actually started talking about his week. You know, like, the hours he spent at the fucking hospital, and an article he read about some black hole void thing eating up some part of the galaxy, and whatever his stupid single mother was up to. I don't want to be rude, it's just, like, tedious. I saw his mum from a distance one time when I left his place and she was fully made up and neurotic skinny. Whatever. All I know is that when he was talking about all of this mundane and irrelevant shit I could barely concentrate. We had this amazing weekend together and now he's acting like it never happened. Fuck. He's probably already seeing someone else. Some other fucking skank probably snagged him during our week off. I know, it's terrible. It's just how shit fucking works, you know? Men can't be with themselves for, like, two seconds. I don't understand how they can keep attracting so many distractions and compartmentalizing their experiences. Women can't. I know that from when I was dating what's-her-name. Everything is more flowy with women, you know? Sure, we might have no boundaries. We're designed to be, like, emotionally unstable, right? I dunno. I'm loving your kimono by the way. Anyway. I feel like, as a woman, everything is holistic, and it flows, and things don't need to be so clearly stated or structured in such a regimented way. So I was, like, dude. Why haven't you contacted me? Yep. I said it. Just like that. My heart was racing so fast! I'm not sure how many drinks I've had. Do you want one? I might get one in a minute. And you know what he said in response? He looked confused and he goes, 'Well, you didn't contact me?' and I was, like, 'Don't play games!' Then he accused *me* of playing games. Man, I think I'm just going to let the whole thing go. I don't have time for people who are so deeply entrenched in emotional and spiritual blockages like that. Let the other skanks have him! Then he was like, 'I thought we were taking time apart to think about what we wanted.' Yeah, he had the fucking audacity to throw that back in my face and before I could say anything, he said that he really liked me. I didn't even know where to start with that one. He can't have it both ways. He must think that I'm stupid or easy or something. He probably just wants to get laid. Guys just go with what's right in front of them, you know? So I played it really cool and I said that it wasn't the time to start using flattery. He'd had all week to do that and he had chosen not to. Boom. Then he pretended like he didn't understand where I was coming from. People and the narratives they cling to! I swear. I need to travel again to get away from all of this shit. I'm over it. Men in this city are suffering from some serious defects. Dating defects! TM! Although, the sex with him was. Fucking. Amazing. That's a whole other brunch date to look forward to! I just...life is too short to spend so much time dealing with people who are on such a different level vibrationally. Like, no judgment, it's just that some of us have cultivated a vibration that's a bit different and a bit higher maybe, and I think he's just a bit below me right now. He's so basic. Maybe that's why he was such a good lover. I wonder how many people he's been with to know how to do all those things that he did. You know how I did that workshop a few months ago? Well, he was the first guy I actually felt comfortable enough to do some of the techniques with. He wasn't freaked out at all! He seemed happy to, like, slow down and touch me in the ways that I would suggest. Oh, man. Sex with that fucking guy. It was mind blowing. Do you think he's good looking? Part of me thought it was sweet that he and his mother clearly have this weekly ritual where she visits him and they have salad together. It's probably the only solid feed she gets all week! She does his washing still, too. He wasn't ashamed of that at all when he told me about it. He said that it's a great way for them to spend time together and that she 'loves' doing it. Like, seriously, dude. Your mum doesn't love you or doing your laundry that much. Get a top loader and grow a pair. Oh, I'm being mean, aren't I? I just don't know what to say to him. I don't know what he wants. I feel, like, used or something. I think he just wants me for the sexuality classes I went to. You throw words like 'sex workshop' around and people just lose their shit. Do you want another drink? I think I'll go in and get one. I just saw him go somewhere and I'm not sure where he is now. Can you be here when I get back? I'm nervous!"

"You're not coming back."

"What?"

"If we're meant to find each other, we will."

"All right, yeah, ok! The universe can guide us, right? You're so wise. Wish me luck!"

"I don't believe in luck!"

22.

My brain wires are fried. I'm definitely going for that walk now. The street seems quiet. There are no stars, and the sun has officially set, and the air is thick and immobilizing. I keep expecting to hear thunder, and I don't. The pressure on my skull is immense, and there aren't enough Christmas lights along this street to distract me. I have very high expectations when it comes to suburbia at Christmas time. I mean, if you're going to have a house, and a family, and a fence, and everything, make the most out of it. Use every socially sanctioned opportunity that you have at your disposal to adorn and celebrate the fact of having it.

This street still has a lot going for it, though. The houses are very eclectic. Most of them are Victorian terrace houses, and Victorian terrace houses are incapable of cultivating any kind of uniformity or predictability. It's like the original aim of consistency in their design led them down this completely unruly and erratic path. Now, they think for themselves. They've seen things, and they know things, and they have different names, and different gardens, and different paint jobs, and different detailing, and different extensions, and different histories.

There's one with an iron gate that's wide open, and the footpath is in the process of being unearthed by what looks like a very insistent and very abundant fig tree. The front door is also open, and a red-and-gold Christmas wreath is hanging across the security door. I can see a hallway, with wooden floors, and a large brown poodle sleeping across them. The lights are on and the sound of classical music is wafting from somewhere down the back of the house.

Number 42 has wind chimes on the veranda and children's bikes strewn across the front porch's tiles. On the upstairs balcony there's a washing line filled with striped pajamas and tiny T-shirts and Spiderman undies. There are succulents lining each of the windowsills, and the front door is shut, with a handmade angel hanging off its knocker. I don't think anybody's home. They're probably at Carols by Candlelight. Or maybe that's tomorrow night.

There's a pool party happening out the back of this next place, which has a very high, and very thick, and very black, and very modern fence around it. It's like a fortress. There's an intercom, too, which I'm going to press, because when I see a button in public, I can't not press it. I can hear pop music and splashing and Marco Polo being played, and I can smell barbecued meats and sweet sauces and cigarette smoke. The adults must be doing the drinking, and the smoking, and the cooking, and the kids must be doing the playing.

The next few houses are silent and still. Most of the blinds are drawn, and there aren't many cars parked on the street. Christmas must have called their tenants elsewhere. There's no moonlight and I've just noticed that there's a guy walking behind me. He's, maybe, three hundred meters away? I don't want to look because that'd give away the fact that I was noticing him and being affected by his presence. Which I am. Yet I don't want him to know that. I don't want to give him the satisfaction. Especially if he's a serial killer, or a rapist, or some sort of sadistic fuck who gets off on freaking people out and my fear is exactly what he wants, or some shit.

So many women living in Melbourne have been murdered in this exact same situation in recent years. One woman died a couple suburbs away from here, and when she did, the sense of safety that I felt in this city really shifted. She was twenty-two, and this guy followed her on foot for a few miles, and then raped her, and strangled her to death in the middle of Princes Park. I can see its treetops from where I'm walking. It was after midnight and she had even texted her boyfriend saying, "almost there," and she never arrived.

Now, whenever I'm walking through the city at night, or I'm going down a darkened street on my own, and I see another woman doing the same, I want to cry. And whenever I see a man, I feel frightened.

I'm also, like, really uncomfortable with people walking behind me. Not just in moments like this, when I'm literally a girl walking alone at night. I'm uncomfortable about it on busy streets, and when I'm wandering around shops, and standing in queues. If I can sense people behind me I get super creeped out. Like, fuck off, you know? My back starts to ache, and my jaw becomes tense, and I want to rip my way out, and roar at everything.

I might cross the road and see what happens. I've always been told to run and hide from scary things and yet, conversely, I'm also supposed to be ready to go into combat with them. Like, somehow, I'm meant to have my keys between my fingers and be feigning confidence right up until the moment when I'm screaming for help.

I also have this terrible habit of becoming so focused on what's frightening me and making me nervous that I can't comprehend anything else. I become mesmerized by it. One time I was driving past a motorcycle accident with a friend and although she couldn't look at the body lying on the ground, I couldn't look away.

Here was a guy wearing a leather motorcycle jacket, with a red stripe across the middle, and thick black jeans, and sneakers. I couldn't see his face, because he still had his helmet on. He was lying on his back, which is better than being on your front, right? And none of his limbs were twisted or mangled or anything. Although, he was very still, and that was a bit unnerving.

Something propels me to face whatever frightens me, no matter how much it hurts, or how much it might adversely affect me. It can take days, weeks, months, or even years to come to terms with what I have seen—and yet I have an insatiable need to see it.

It's scary, because anything could be done to me, and I'll always want to watch it unfold. I'll want to take in every detail and find a way to come to terms with it, and to understand it. I have a need to find "helpful lessons" in everything I encounter and I often fear that I'll be unable to say "no" or "stop" when I need to, because I'm always just . . . watching. I worry that I'll never be able to hold someone else one hundred percent accountable for anything.

Like, I could be stabbed multiple times, and I swear to god I will hear myself thinking, "Fascinating, fascinating, I wonder what has driven them to this, and what I represent to them, and what they must be going through to have taken such a drastic action, and could I ever imagine doing the same? How have I attracted this? What is this going to mean for my life, and soul, and all of the things that I am destined to learn? And I certainly didn't expect the sensation of being stabbed to be like getting my ears pierced, where there isn't really any pain, just a strong awareness of something penetrating me and piercing my flesh? Wow."

I stay with what hurts, and I'm often the last one standing.

23.

He's still behind me, I think. It's a bit too shadowy back there to be able to tell. I'm just going to keep moving, because I'm not sure if there's room to transmute anything into love, or into empathy. Most of the time that's deemed to be "dangerous" and "silly" and "idealistic" anyway. Plus I don't know how to create space for it mentally when I'm freaking out. I once read this book about how to non-violently communicate, and it talked about how to do so in high-stakes situations, and I can't remember what it said now.

He's crossed the road. Great. I've got another full street length and a bit to go before I've done the whole block and I'm back at the party. If he gets too close, I'll go straight into someone's front yard and ring the doorbell. Or, I'll knock. Like, really loudly.

In moments like this I often wonder what would happen if Crime Stoppers wasn't about catching criminals after the fact. What if it was actually about catching them beforehand. Like, what if we could call Crime Stoppers when we felt ourselves potentially about to commit a crime? I can imagine feeling very scared before committing a crime. There must be millions of tiny decisions and warning signs that lead up to the point of finally acting it out. Imagine if one of those tiny decisions could be, "Oh, shit, yeah, I'd better call Crime Stoppers, I think I'm about to do something potentially violent and/or dangerous because I can't see a way out," and then the police's job would be to chuck us into counseling, or into rehab, for a certain period of time, depending upon the potential offense.

It could be like Suicide Watch, except we'd Crime Watch ourselves, and each other, and make sure that we're all ok, and if shit gets hectic we could go to therapy. I guess therapy and rehab aren't the answer to everything. Ashrams and meditation retreats and health spas are pretty powerful, too. And I suppose there's no guarantee that we still wouldn't commit the crime.

Yet imagine a system that could provide this amazing stopgap where everyone became involved in the prevention of crime, rather than just catching and punishing criminals. It could seriously save the world, dissolve all of the stigmas around criminals and the ways in which they're dehumanized. It could totally revolutionize the prison system. Like, what prison system, you know? It'd be a *therapy* system. Then potential victims could be notified, and families and friends who are concerned about loved ones could call in, and businesses being targeted could be alerted as to what's happening, and everyone could get a memo or whatever.

That guy is still just walking along at this infuriatingly casual pace. I don't know what to make of it. One time a guy chased me down a street a lot like this one very late at night and he was yelling, "Hey, bitch! I just want to talk to you! I won't lay a hand on you!" and I wanted to stop, turn around, look him in the face, and say, "Look, dude. You've won. You've conquered. You're the man. I'm yours. Sold! For Fear Of My Own Life! And Of What You Might Do To My Physical Body! And For All The Years of Rehabilitation That Will Inevitably Follow This Harrowing Experience! Take me, I'm yours. What's the use in fighting it? Ah. You just wanted the thrill of the chase. I see. How primitive. Well, despite everything that's led to your chasing me, and wanting to scare me, and grab me, and possess me, and rip me to pieces, and maybe kill me, there's still holiness in you. Yep. You and I are both more than this moment. Neither of us can ever be truly maimed or destroyed. Not really. What's led us both here, and what will continue leading us elsewhere, is just a spiral of energy, churning and whirling into infinity. We can choose to take responsibility for that. I mean, we can wake up to the power that we have right here, in this moment, and we can make a choice that points us in a different direction from the one we're headed right now. We can connect to the fact that there's more than this, and that *we're* so much more than this. Or not. It's up to us. Whaddya say?"

I kept running, though, because that's what you're supposed to do. I evaded the guy, and all of the demons that came with him, and, because of that, I became the hero of my own story. Well, not really. He still haunts me. I didn't really escape him.

I mean, he's following me right now. Every step that I take, he takes one, too.

And I would rather die than run again. I've become, like, morally opposed to running away because I don't want to spread fear and I don't want there to be anything to run from. "Running" from another human being doesn't even make sense.

I want to be able to look everyone on this planet in the fucking face and if that means looking death in the fucking face, then so be it. We all have to look it in the face eventually. It can't be as bad as everyone makes it out to be. I mean, the way in which we die could be violent, or unexpected, or tragic, or whatever. Yet death in-and-of-itself is just what it is, and I don't think it means any harm.

Fearing death seems like such a limited, earth-bound, mortal thing. Not a universal, intergalactic, expansive, infinite thing.

After reading all of these ancient Egyptian texts, and absorbing their attitudes toward life and death and the underworld and the afterlife, my perspective on my own so-called demise completely changed. I even studied Cleopatra and committed suicide in front of an acting class, and when I came out the other side, I understood that death doesn't even exist. Not in the way that we think it does. It's just been turned into this high and mighty omniscient force that we're supposed to succumb to, and be scared of, and controlled by.

Yet death unites us in the same way that birth does. It's something that we all have in common. It's a part of us. It's a doorway, and just because we don't understand what's in the next room, it doesn't mean that there isn't a next room, or that the next room is something to be scared of. It just means that we haven't been into it before. Or maybe we have, and we just can't remember.

Besides. We don't just go from living to dead and that's it. We keep going. Whenever those I love have died they've gotten bigger somehow. Not smaller. They haven't just disappeared. Even if I've missed their physical forms, and I've grieved the loss of them, they've remained with me. To this day I can still see, smell, and sense those in my life who have died. I can still think their thoughts, and hear their voices, and touch their skin, and feel their feelings. I can still empathize with their yearnings, and frustrations, and connect with their wants, and needs, and aches, and pains. Where does that fit into the narrative of dying and leaving everything and everyone forever? Yeah. It doesn't.

Nothing and no one ever leaves. Not really. We just change form. I'm dying and being reborn all of the time. I swear I've already died, like, several times tonight. Like, the baby version of me has died, and the toddler version of me has died, and the little child version of me has died, and the adolescent version of me has died, and the person I was earlier tonight has died. Not because she wasn't "good enough" or because she "sinned" or because she needed to be "improved" or "punished." More because it was her inherent nature to die and to be reborn over and over and over again.

Oh, wow. Look at this fucking epic house! There's a neon nativity scene out front! And there are fairy lights hanging from the roof like a waterfall! It's raining fucking Christmas lights.

Oh my goddess. I've never seen anything like it. Holy shit, there's even a Magen David! On the top of the roof, there's like, an attic, and they've put this massive, hot-pink, neon Magen David on the top. Like a cherry. Or maybe it's a pentagram? Whatever. The fence around the property is low, and made of brick, and it's lit up with little lights. I might sit down. Yes, I feel propelled to sit down. This could be one of the stupidest and most unsafe decisions that I've ever made, and yet, I'm going to make it. If there was ever a place to die, it would be right here, in front of neon Jesus, and neon Mary, and neon Joseph, and all of the neon Wise Men, and the cute little neon animals.

24.

That guy has gone and I'm not sure whether I feel relieved or considerably more freaked out. Could he be hiding somewhere? Like, behind a hedge or fence, or down a driveway? That'd be a pretty extreme length to go to. Whatever, universe. I refuse to believe that the lesson of this experience is "don't walk alone at night" or "don't walk alone at night without telling anyone" because having to report my whereabouts to I-don't-know-who around the clock kind of minimizes the multidimensional nature of my existence, and positions life in a slightly more dystopian reality than the one I'd ideally like to live in. I mean, that woman's boyfriend knew exactly where she was and that didn't stop what happened from happening to her.

25.

Walking through the front gate of the party feels so satisfying now. It's like I've finally reached safety after a long, perilous journey. I really want to tell somebody about the semi-traumatizing and totally revelatory experience that I've just had, and yet there's no one to tell. I mean, there are heaps of people to tell, and yet there's no one to tell. I'm weaving between them all and avoiding eye contact, because if I happened to lock eyes with somebody, they'd see that I had something to say, and that'd be embarrassing, because I wouldn't say it.

It's just that so much good came from my going for a walk. Some of my fears were turned into joy, and love, and miracles, and neon lights. When people ask me what I "do," I often say that I'm an alchemist, because it seems to be the most honest label to put on all the things I don't want to be labeled as. It makes sense to me. Although, it wouldn't to my dad. I'm always conscious of what would or wouldn't make sense to my dad. He's like an inbuilt judicial system, governing my every move, and thought, and feeling, and choice.

And when I use the word *alchemist* to describe myself, I'm fully aware that Dad would think this was a bit "smart," and a bit "cute," and maybe a bit of an indication that I was leaning on the philosophies of my therapist a tad too much. Dad preferred that I lean on him, and his philosophies, rather than on those of other people. So while he encouraged me to have an open mind, and to become my own person, and to think for myself, he was very wary about the person I was becoming, and the people I was listening to.

He believed that the purpose of words and labels was to make things clearer, not more complex and diverse. To him, words and labels were there to organize, and to categorize, and to serve an objective reality that we could all trust and accept. Yet it always seemed to me that if there's an objective reality that we all share, it has to be wordless.

Because everyone has such an individualized relationship with words, and with labels. No matter how "conventional" or "traditional" or "widely accepted" we might perceive our choice of words or labels to be, our interpretations are subjective. Like, when I tell someone that I'm a stripper, or a painter, or a stockbroker, or even an alchemist, it unlocks a whole kaleidoscope of experiences and impressions inside of them that aren't mine, and that have nothing to do with me, and that I have absolutely no control over. They might love strippers, or they might judge them harshly. They might be besties with a stockbroker, or they might have lost all of their earnings to one.

I tried to address this with Dad, and he said that I should go and study linguistics before putting my case to him. He hadn't studied linguistics. He just thought that I should. I doubt that he would have then wanted me to teach him about linguistics. He just thought that I should learn about linguistics before raising the subject with him.

26.

I'm moving toward the living room and saying a prayer for my past self—the one that was frightened—and saying one for the guy I believed to be following me. I forgive you and I release you. I forgive you and I release you. I forgive you and I release you.

Prayers aren't reserved for those who regularly go to church, or to a synagogue, or to a mosque, or wherever. Prayers are for everyone. Even spells and curses aren't just for those who own cauldrons, or broomsticks, or crystal balls. We're all saying prayers and casting spells with our words, and our thoughts, and where we point our fingers.

I know, because I worked in a magic shop once, and I learned about it. The woman who owned the place was in insurance for forty years before she became a witch and started getting into some seriously freaky shit. Whenever things would go badly for her, she'd assume that somebody, somewhere, had cast a spell. Paranoia and suspicion came very naturally, which was probably the perfect disposition for working in insurance, yet it wasn't ideal for a self-professed healer and "empath."

She had immaculately groomed long white hair, and blood-red nails, and she was highly cryptic about everything, from her thoughts and feelings to her intentions. The ingredients that went into all of the potions that she sold, in all of these little brown glass vials, were swathed in secrecy. I remember saying to her that people might enjoy learning about what went into her "Love Potions" and "Abundance Oils" and she laughed, and grinned, and declared that, yes, people would probably enjoy "stealing her magic." She didn't trust anyone, and she frequently created experiences affirming the ways in which she must never trust anyone.

Another esoteric shop opened up down the street and she firmly believed that they were out to get her. Despite all of the evidence to suggest that *she* was out to get her. She was cursing and spelling herself constantly. She mustn't have read the section in those Witchy books that deals with that. Because when I did, while working on the desk, I noticed that all of the books said whatever you send out comes back to you multiplied. Like, Witchy-Ness-101: Don't put curses or nasty spells on other people, or assume the worst about them, because you're really spelling, and cursing, and creating the worst for yourself.

One day she asked me to polish every last rune and piece of jewelry filling the glass cabinets that were located across the premises, and it involved me literally having to squat down on the floor, and scrub. As I was halfway through doing this, she walked through the room and mused, "Oh! There's no need to kneel before me as I pass," and I got up, walked out, and never went back.

Apparently, she was furious. Parting ways with someone or something doesn't always make sense, so people often create reasons to be angry and resentful, because it weaves a stronger narrative around the process of letting go. That way, they don't have to take responsibility for their part in it, because, you know. So-and-so was just a bitch and shit.

All of the fairies and crystal healers and shamans and palm readers that worked out of the shop instructed me to do cord-cutting rituals, and to visualize white light coming from the earth, and through my body, and up into the cosmos, in order to protect myself from her spells, and voodoo vibes. The only problem was that through them telling me to do this they manifested a way for me, and for them, to continue feeling frightened of her.

And I refused to give that druid-pagan-witch-lady-empath—or whatever she wants to call herself now that she's living off her super—the satisfaction of my fear. I'd seen *Star Wars* and I knew that I was the force, and that the force was with me, and that my words and thoughts were mine, and that they couldn't be hijacked or influenced by a bitter woman and her ridiculous "magicks."

No matter how scary or intimidating a person may appear to be, we don't need to "protect" ourselves from them. As long as we can turn our experiences into love, there's no need to waste time and energy being frightened, or trying to stop things and people from coming in or going out.

27.

This living room is more like a dying room. There's a small window looking out at a wooden fence, and an ice-blue plastic Christmas tree, lit up and sitting on the floor in one of the corners. There's an enormous TV that's turned off, and a turntable that isn't playing, and a massive pair of speakers presiding over the entire space like obelisks. There are heaps of people dancing, and the music that they've put on is electro. A few guys are sprawled across the couches, stoned, staring blankly at the dancing people, whom I might join.

The members of the group that are closest to the door are tanned to perfection, evenly, all over, like the roast chickens Dad used to cook with Vegemite. They're wearing variations on the same theme: denim cut-offs, tiny vests, different combinations of swimwear, body glitter, feathers, piercings, headbands, floral wreaths, and headscarves. I can't wear headbands or headscarves, because if I don't have air around my head I feel like I've died.

I've kept moving because I want to find a spot in the room that allows me to let loose without having to interact with anyone too directly. I like dancing for dancing's sake. It's a break from having to participate in verbal communication, which always seems to be about explaining shit, and proving shit, and clarifying shit, and arguing about shit, and criticizing shit, and showing off about shit, and avoiding shit, and dramatizing shit, and cracking jokes about shit, and brushing shit off, and defending shit, and attacking shit, and lying about shit, and insisting that shit will be "ok," when truly empathizing and connecting with people involves feeling everything, and saying nothing.

I find that I have a much deeper appreciation for my fellow human beings when their mouths are shut. So dancing at a party provides an opportunity to connect with a room full of people, without having to say a word to them.

It's hot in here, though, so I might move closer to the window. It's closed. I'll try to open it. Oh, no. It's painted shut. Let's pretend that my attempt to open it didn't happen. If anyone noticed they'd probably be like, "What's that chick doing in here if she just wants to get out?" And I'd reply, "Yes, well, I'm often asking myself the same thing."

The people in this part of the room have adopted more of a bondage vibe. They're wearing over-the-knee platform boots, and leather straps with buckles across their bodies, and chokers, and wigs, and black lipstick. They're dancing with each other in very fleshy ways. Two of them have toy guns that are shooting bubbles.

I can also see a handful of sweaty guys sifting around in oversized band T-shirts with tracksuit pants, and floppy hair, and thin gold chains around their necks. One of them is wearing a dangly earring in one ear, and a pre-rolled cigarette behind the other. I think that they're trying to be stealth as they blatantly check everyone else out. We have something in common. Although, they seriously look like they could be trying to steal some shit. Woe the person with the ever-so-slightly open backpack or bumbag. A handful of girls swaddled in tie-dye T-shirt dresses and puka shell necklaces also seem suspicious. Or maybe they just want to interact with them. It's hard to tell.

There are a couple of dudes wearing enormous wings making out really intensely in the middle of the room, and a whole bunch of women lined up along one of the walls wearing chunky sneakers, sports socks, silky run shorts, crop tops, and midriff-exposing hoodies—which I didn't know existed—and long, fluorescent acrylic nails. They aren't dancing. For some reason they're in here trying to talk with one another, and every time they go to say something, they raise their hands to their mouths and the diamantes on the tips of their nails shimmer in the darkness.

Everyone looks as if they've just gotten back from a trip to a beach, or to a lake, or to a music festival, where they're supposed to dress and act like they've connected with tribal values, and with each other, and with their bodies, and with nature, even though they haven't. Not really.

They were too busy trying to find the people that they went with, and trying to get phone reception, and trying to catch a glimpse of the person with the drugs, and trying to spot famous people, and trying to find a food stall with less expensive nachos, and trying to sneak into sectioned-off VIP areas, and trying to move their campsite closer to the main stage, and trying to spew, and trying to sleep, and trying to have an experience other than the one that they were actually having.

Or maybe the people in here have merely perfected the art of looking like they've been to a beach, or to a lake, or to a music festival, when they've really just spent the week checking their inboxes, and attending meetings, because their job description has "marketing" at the start and "communications" in the middle and something to do with "consulting" at the end.

It's more fashionable to seem like something than to actually be something. That way, everyone can appear to be living a life of vitality and autonomy, without actually having to. They can just work like slaves, and occasionally dress up in the latest trends, and make "beats," and go to festivals, and put the work of artists who have chosen to be "courageous" and "original" beside their own, because they think that by association they'll seem more "courageous" and "original" themselves.

The only problem is that to be "courageous" and "original," you actually have to be "courageous" and "original," and if you spend too much time and energy trying to appear as though you're "courageous" and "original" you become so invested in the appearance of being it, that you can never actually be it.

28.

I found a good spot near the Christmas tree, which most people seem to be avoiding. Although, there's a girl to my left wearing a lacy pastel-pink negligee, and pigtails, and she's started swaying her hips in the exact same way that I am swaying my hips, and she keeps looking over here at my swaying hips like she's studying them. She's with a friend who seems to be very distracted, and who is also in a silky negligee, just with less lace. And it's an olive-green color.

She and I haven't even made eye contact. She's just quietly going about observing my movement, and learning it, and minding her own business, which is to make my business her business. Copying others must make her feel more at ease, and I get that. I just couldn't do what she's doing without being fully aware of the fact that I was doing it, and then I'd have to share with the person I was copying that I was copying them. Like, "Yeah, I know, I'm mimicking you in order to feel safe! Hope that's chill!"

I feel out of place in here. Everyone has multiples of themselves and it's making me nervous. My presence messes with the established hierarchy. Before I came along, their mirror neurons were firing away happily, and now, people are awkwardly looking and not looking at me, and other people are starting to notice. Oh, well. I'm just going to close my eyes and witness shit.

So there's the music, and the room, and the space beyond the room, and the mind, and the body, and the breath, and the spirit, and then my relationship to the music, and to the room, and to the space beyond the room, and to the mind, and to the body, and to the breath, and to the spirit, and now everything beyond the room, and the mind, and the body, and the breath, and the spirit. And the moon, I can feel the moon.

The other night I had this dream about a really authoritative woman who was making her way around a large crowd of people, and I could sense that she was important, because everyone was responding to her in a way that made themselves seem small. They were widening their eyes, and doing fluttery things with their breath, and making frantic, tight, gossipy little gestures, and carefully watching her every move, before consorting with each other, and smirking.

She requested that those who were trained dancers make themselves known, and do a demonstration for her. I wasn't trained, so I didn't draw attention to myself. Yet she stood next to me and demanded that I dance for her, and, to my surprise, rather than feeling humiliated, it felt humbling to have been asked to do so. I didn't know the correct movements, or timing, or anything. I just rolled my wrists around my body, and up over my head, as I swished my hips from side to side, and oxygen started going to places inside of me that it hadn't been to before. There was nothing to stop me, and I had nothing to lose, because I wasn't trained, anyway. I wasn't schooled in anything. There were no rules. It was just me, and whatever came out.

I'm about to cry, so I'll keep my eyes closed. Dancing with strangers is one thing. Crying and dancing with them is quite another. Most people aren't cognizant of the fact that, in order to feel comfortable, they require others not to cry or do anything outside of the established code of conduct, which is an unspoken code of conduct, of course. Nevertheless, it must be adhered to, and implemented, through harnessing certain movements and non-invasive forms of eye contact, and it doesn't come naturally to me, nor does it tend to involve crying unexpectedly.

Rather, it involves dancing in a slightly more reserved way, and occasionally meeting the gaze of different people, and staying glued to the one spot because, when it comes down to it, everyone would rather that I not be here. They're merely tolerating my presence, and I mustn't test the boundaries of that. I'm an outsider, and I must act like I know it.

That said, I do get tired of having to "earn my keep" everywhere I go. Sometimes I just want to *be* with other people. I can't ever recall moving my body exactly the way I wanted to, or looking exactly where I was drawn to, or saying exactly what I felt compelled to, or crying exactly when I needed to, in a social situation.

Dad always encouraged me to adapt and to do what others expected, and to say please and thank you and hello and goodbye, and to prioritize others' feelings and preferences over my own. Telling this to a child who was equipped to develop a fixed identity, or persona, might have been helpful. I can see how a child naturally drawn to putting themselves first might have benefited from a father who was telling them to care more about other people. It just so happens that I have no idea who I am, and I read somewhere that women have no fixed identity at all, which is why it's always being fought over and debated.

I'm constantly in a philosophical dialectic with Dad in my head about this. He based his identity on what he "should" or "should not" be doing. He was raised a Catholic, and he justified his and other people's behavior based on whether or not it was something that "should" or "should not" be done, like one of the Ten Commandments. He exercised daily because he "should," and he called his sister back because he "should," and he paid his bills on time because he "should," and he lived, worked, and breathed because he "should."

Considering who he was, or what he truly wanted, wasn't really something that he "should" be doing. So he would lecture Mum and me on "shoulds" and "shouldn'ts" over the dinner table each night until she would quietly down some diazepam and go to bed, and I wouldn't eat until midday the next day.

The sheer force of his "shoulds" spun our reality, and our feelings didn't really have a place in it.

Whenever I questioned what he said, or I chose to remain silent, or I tried to argue, or I cried, he'd tell me that I "shouldn't" be arguing, or that I "should" be saying something, or that I "shouldn't" be crying, or that I "should" apologize, and then he'd say that he was sorry, and that he loved me. Probably because he "should."

29.

Right near one of the speakers there's a woman wearing perfectly fitted, high-waisted cream linen trousers, and a stringy cream-colored bikini top, and spongy cream sneakers, and everyone seems to be very aware of her. When she's not looking at them, they're looking at her, and when she's looking at them, they're looking at her. There's no escape. She's a very glossy and very creamy individual. There are dimples on either side of her smile. Her hair is long and wavy. It's dripping down her back like caramel.

She isn't actively doing anything to warrant so much attention. She isn't being rowdy, or dancing especially enthusiastically. She's just swaying, and being seen. Swaying, and being seen. She's just existing, and people are doing the rest of the work for themselves. Because those who are seen to be physically perfect, symmetrical, handsome, and beautiful by society's standards are here to show us how to feel compassion for ourselves, while those who have physical difficulties are here to show us how to feel compassion for others.

She just whispered in the ear of the guy beside her, and then laughed, and her laughter shot around the room like an electrical circuit. The recipient of the "joke" didn't do so well. His simulated laugh was below par. He did this very insecure and un-ironic sideways movement with his eyes so as to gauge everyone else's reaction to what had just happened, probably because his way of measuring the validity, or morality, of any given situation is to assess the nature of everyone else's responses to it. He doesn't know how anything truly makes him feel, or how a woman like her makes him feel, because he's never stopped to think about it. His feelings don't matter to him. What everyone *else* thinks matters to him. Which is probably why he's talking to her. She's everything that he "should" be talking to. Culturally, she fits the bill. Which is perfect, because now he can use her to compete for status among his mates.

He's wearing camos and combat boots, and dark tendrils of hair are being pushed out of his eyes by a thin black headband. His outfit is probably supposed to exude some sort of militant authoritarian vibe, and yet he doesn't seem militant or authoritarian at all. He seems lost, and out of control. He's tall, and fumbly, and every time he goes to say something, his chest caves in and his posture crumbles. He must have been a massive kid with sticky fingers and a red face who got teased by everybody and then went through a crazy growth spurt, and now, even as a grown man, he doesn't know what to do with all of his limbs.

She keeps calling his eyes to different parts of her body through playing with her hair, and fiddling with her bikini straps, and tilting her head one way and then the other, and putting her hands on her hips. The tan lines across her back are glowing in the dark. The volume of the music is supporting whatever it is that she wants to create with him, too, because they keep having to lean in closer to hear each other.

Ah! She just showed him her tattoo. Classic. Drawing attention to this required that she twist her torso, slightly, and invite his gaze into her side-boob, and ribs, and stomach, in a very direct way, because the tattoo was situated along her side. It's a crescent moon, I think. Perfect. His gaze was then forced deeper into her physical person and down into all of the places that she can sense he has forbidden for himself.

People are obsessed with what they don't allow themselves to have, and then they become controlled by it. Forbidden fruit is everyone's main meal. I allow myself to have everything, so I cannot be controlled. Dad found the boundlessness of my curiosity to be a living, breathing attack on his person. It splintered every idea that he had about himself, and the world.

There's a photograph of the two of us when I was four or five, which Mum took when we were staying at a Victorian-era hotel by the beach in Queenscliff. We'd just had a buffet breakfast in the courtyard, and we went to look at different rooms of the building, and I remember Dad insisting that I not touch any of the furniture, or get it dirty. I'm not sure how

I would've gotten it dirty. It's not like I'd gone out and rolled around in the sand dunes between taking sips of pulpy fresh OJ, and shoveling mouthfuls of flaky croissant in my gob. I mean, I was wearing my favorite red-and-white polka-dot dress, and my Mary Janes, and my frilly ankle socks, because I was in a special place, having a special time with my mum and dad.

So, naturally, for the purposes of the photo, I lay back on a pink-and-gold chaise lounge and defiantly thrust my strong little legs in the air, miles away from the seat, and shook them about, as my father sat in the background, legs tightly crossed, whitened knuckles wrapped around the arms of his chair, as if he were steering a ship that was veering wildly and frighteningly off course.

For his birthday one year I turned that photo into a bookmark, and he never used it. I put sparkles on it and not even glitter could make that particular dynamic between us safe or humorous for him.

My mother was far better skilled at giving Dad the impression that our family was a benign dictatorship, and that he was at the head of it. He saw her as a saint, and she accomplished saintly status through numbing out, and staying relatively silent, and manifesting migraines, which would force her to take a cocktail of drugs, and spend days sleeping in darkened rooms with heavy curtains.

Living with Mum was like living with a vault that got a kick out of the sound of itself sealing shut. She preferred it when others miraculously managed to guess her wants and needs.

That way, she didn't have to go through the arduous process of having to articulate or fight for them herself.

I'd have dreams about what I was supposed to do or not do for her, which primed me for living in a constant state of tension around most people. Especially women. Because whatever the fuck seems to be happening isn't happening, and whatever's actually happening isn't either, according to them.

You can be speaking with a woman about a seemingly innocuous subject, be it politics, movies, friends, work, relationships, food, tattoos, weather, astrology, pets, rent, crystals, tarot, or whatever, and the whole thing can become very highly charged, very quickly, because the subtext is actually something other than what's being said. What's actually being said is about seduction, competition, secrecy, power, security, inclusion, exclusion, sex, weakness, strength, or addiction.

It's difficult for women to be honest and direct because for centuries we were burned at the stake, or persecuted, or exiled, or rejected, or excommunicated, or divorced, or shamed, or socially excluded, for saying what we truly thought and felt. Now, we know how to act like we're being direct and forthright, when we're not, and we know how to seem uninhibited and free, when we're not, and we know how to appear helpless and damaged, when we're not. Deception is more ingrained in us than honesty.

Mum got on famously with women who manipulated outcomes through playing the role of the victim. Her closest friends were always unwell, and suffering from all manner of diseases, and court cases, and low self-esteem issues, and substance abuse problems, and jobs that didn't fulfill them, and employers and family members taking them for granted.

They'd say that they were amenable and adaptable, when they weren't. Not really. And Mum adored this. She'd be like, "Oh, so-and-so would never ask, because she's a sweetie, however, it'd really nice if you did X, Y, or Z for her."

She'd describe her friends as being "gorgeous" and "lovely" and "such darlings" because it was always: oh, no, you go first. Oh, no, I can change my plans. Oh, no, it's all yours. Oh, no, don't worry about it! In the hopes that, actually, you would let them go first, and you would change your plans, and it would be all theirs, and you would worry about it, because when you went first, and when you didn't change your plans, and when it was all yours, and when you didn't worry about them, they hated you. They hated you with a resentment so intense that it had the capacity to become malignant and cancerous for us all.

Mum was ashamed of my honesty and directness. She never saw it as gorgeous, or as sweet, or as just darling. She found it "confusing" and "confounding." She would sit back and sip her drink and commend me for my "ambitiousness" and "drive." I wasn't ambitious or driven. I just knew what I wanted, and I wasn't afraid to ask for it.

Although, there have been times in my life when I've known exactly what I would need to do, or say, in order to maneuver someone in such a way so as to get exactly what I thought I wanted out of them, without having to state anything directly. It's like a sixth sense.

I once had to stop dating a guy because I realized that he

only spent time with me when I behaved in needy and overly attentive ways toward him. The largely unfulfilling relationship that we had could have continued if I were lonely enough, and desperate enough, to force it to do so. I mean, this method was working for a whole bunch of other women. His ex-girlfriend was constantly calling him, and rocking up at his house unannounced, and he was heading overseas with an older woman who had bought him a ticket, and no, she knew nothing about me, or his ex, and nor was she his current girlfriend, who visited him at work each day with a thermos full of pumpkin soup.

He refused to take responsibility for his life, so others happily did.

30.

Ayaayyy! That woman just touched that guy on the arm and it sent another wave of shock around the room. He can't hold his ground at all. He isn't accustomed to being the center of attention. He fears it, and he craves it. She understands this, and knows very well that she must occasionally say "no" to him, and scold him, in order to give him the impression that a "chase" is occurring for the sake of his ego.

She keeps rolling her eyes, and poking him, and dismissing the things that he says via shrugging her shoulders, and waving him away with her hand, and raising her eyebrows in disbelief, like, "What? You can't be serious, dude."

She's criticizing him, and making him feel small every now and then, so that he believes that he has to work hard for her approval. Then he can fool himself into thinking that he's "conquering" her, and she can receive a perverse satisfaction out of undermining his capabilities and his manhood, because it gives her a false sense of certainty about her own womanhood.

And, no, I don't think she's about to go home, and honor her feelings, and have a cry, and reflect on her communication style, and its ramifications. Crying and reflecting is most likely a problem for her. It's an admission of feeling something, and maybe having made a mistake, and she can't afford to feel feelings or to make mistakes. They're obstacles in the way of her getting what she thinks she wants.

I wonder how long it's been since some warm, relieving tears ran down her cherubim cheeks. Maybe the last time she cried was a performance for a man. Geez. That's always a nasty one. See! Look what you did to me! Another fucking guy who can't fucking be trusted! Fuck you! I'm fucking crazy and it's all your fucking fault! See! I'm crying now! Isn't that crazy! Aren't I a psycho!? Blah!

His body language is beginning to take on a slightly reserved demeanor. His arms have crossed over his heart, and his legs are taking up a wider stance, and he's making less eye contact with her in an attempt to regain territory in a communication where he clearly has none.

Occasionally, he displays a smile so self-deprecating and desperate that I feel a bit violated myself. He's completely deconstructing under the weight of her attention. Others are vying for it, too. People are so attracted to what harms them. Being infatuated, and obsessed, and jealous, and tormented, and competitive, and longing for things, and wanting to possess people, and dying and killing for love, is deemed to be romantic, and sensual, and liberated. Yuck.

Hell is on earth. We create it. It isn't some faraway place that we get sent to once life is over, and we're being punished for all of our crimes, and indiscretions. Our crimes and indiscretions *are* the punishment. Anything that makes us feel shitty, and comes from a shitty place, and inevitably leads to the expansion of shitty-ness, is hell. Just as anything that gives us meaning, and comes from a meaningful place, and inevitably leads to the expansion of meaningfulness, is heaven.

Nevertheless, when I wouldn't participate in psychological and emotional warfare with one boyfriend, he thought that I was a bit naïve and a bit inexperienced. It was endearing for him at first, and then he got impatient, and chose to get his need for co-dependency and toxicity met elsewhere. And I watched.

He surrounded himself with women who held strong opinions about things, and who regularly demanded that he "help" them with their "problems" and play the role of "confidante," which he prided himself on. He adored "being there" for them, and when I shared that I felt lonely in our relationship—because he never expressed his own thoughts or feelings—he told me that no one had ever noticed this before.

One night we went to the theater with his woman friends and saw this very non-verbal and very physical performance piece by Adena Jacobs, which explored women's bodies, and their relationships to them. It left me speechless. I couldn't keep up with the demands of the largely unfulfilling intellectual debate that the women were participating in afterward, seemingly for the benefit of the man present.

I felt embarrassed on his behalf. I don't want to believe that women change their behavior for men, or that men change their behavior for women. Yet, unfortunately, a desire for something not to be true doesn't change the fact that it *might* be true, and I know in my heart that, if he hadn't been there, the nature of the discussion would've been very, very different.

These women seemed to want it both ways: to be respected and seen as thinkers and to also be deemed fragile and incapable because, surely, a man wants all of that, and more, and what he wants matters more than anything.

So I sat there, quietly sipping my martini, unable to stop thinking about all of the things that he had told me he was busy "helping" each of them with: destructive drug habits, issues with their weight, and with their mothers, and with their ex-boyfriends, and with their colleagues, and with their older lovers, and with their siblings.

One of the women was an embittered thirty-something-year-old actress who wore a tiny fitted blazer, and drank more than everyone else, and gazed at my partner through thick eyeliner as she readjusted her low neckline with the carefully manicured fingers of her left hand, and moved her long, sleek, black, shiny hair out of her eyes with the carefully manicured fingers of her right hand.

Later that night, when we were walking home, he told me that if we weren't together, he'd definitely be fucking her. Like, definitely.

We went out to brunch the next day because of course we did, and I told him that I knew very well he believed me to be less intelligent than his woman friends. He clasped his hands together in his signature deeply-and-meaningfully-listening-counselor-daddy-brother-guru-lover-killer position, looked at me over his quinoa porridge, and said, "They've got IQ. You've got EQ."

Whatever *that* means.

31.

I feel lightheaded. My kimono is sticking to the skin at my lower back and around my waist. There are hairs wet with sweat clinging to the base of my neck, and my thighs are dripping inside the spandex. In my mind's eye, I'm wearing golden armor, adorned with roses, and I'm riding a winged horse, and I can feel the wind on my face, and I can smell seawater in the air, and I'm wielding an enormous electric-blue sword, which is cutting through all of the delusions, and lies, and I'm galloping, and galloping, and slicing, and slicing.

Another woman just came up to that guy, and held him by the shoulder, and whispered something in his ear. He nodded without looking at her and there was this frequency of intimacy and familiarity that stopped everything in its tracks. The other woman acted like the interruption hadn't happened, and that it hadn't affected her, or been an obstruction to her efforts. Yet it had.

Now she's breathing really shallowly, and trying not look at him as he's saying good-bye to her, and kissing her on the cheek, in this really awkward and rigid way, because I think that that other woman is his partner, and they're leaving now. What. Why was he talking to her for so long, and in such an intense way? Was he just being "nice" because he'd like to think that he's concerned about "hurting her feelings" when, really, he's just obsessed with making sure that everybody likes him, because he's terrified of being human, and flawed, and real, and complex, and a bit unlikable on occasion? Did he think that she might be a good lay one day, and he wants to keep her hanging around for that? Or did he just want everyone else to *see* him talking to her? Or did he simply reduce what was occurring between them to "nothing" so as to give himself the illusion of self-preservation, and healthy boundaries, seemingly oblivious to the fact that he was giving off wildly mixed messages, and being super-leaky?

I feel bad for her. I read somewhere that most women lose their train of thought, or turn to mush, when a man that they find physically attractive approaches them, or talks to them, or walks into a room. I wish I knew what that felt like. I won't notice a man unless I sense a fifth-dimensional connection to him and to his soul. If I can't see pyramids or past lives with him—or some kind of rope extending from my heart to his—I won't see him.

I once dated a guy who got so much attention for his physical appearance that I started to think there was something wrong with him. People kept congratulating me for "getting" him and for "training him so well" and they'd ask me "what it was like to be with him" and "how I had done it" and "why couldn't he be nice to everyone?" as if we were in Medieval Europe and the last prince of the royal bloodline was now betrothed to me.

I've been in the presence of women who'll see someone they consider to be "good looking" and they'll say things like, "I'd love to ride that" or "Imagine being on the receiving end of that gaze every day" or "I think I just slid off my chair" or "Who is he here with?" or "So dreamy" and I've smiled like an idiot in an attempt to seem simpatico with something that makes absolutely no sense to me.

I want to go over to her and say something. It's just that whenever I speak directly with someone about what's happening in a social situation, they usually deny that anything is happening at all. Or, they acknowledge some truth to what I've observed, before proceeding to say: it's none of your business / do I know you / you're too sensitive / you're brutal / you're paranoid / I was just being friendly / you're upset because you're not the center of attention / I can't go anywhere / I can't talk to anyone / what the fuck / what's the problem / why can't you just take a joke / it was nothing / what are you talking about / why do you always do this / mind your own business.

None of which answers my question, or deals with what I have witnessed. Then I'm left with the something that was, in fact, happening, and no, I don't feel comfortable with it, because no one ever seems to want to see or take responsibility for it, and I have no idea what to do with it. I don't want it, and

I don't understand why I have it. Then I have to let it wash over me, and I start imagining slicing through things with swords, because despite the fact there are people all around, doing all of the things that people do, none of it can be spoken of, or bear to know its own name.

32.

The music is relentless, and heavy, and it's pummeling me, and I'm becoming it, and allowing it to absorb everything that I don't know what to do with, and that doesn't have a place in this room.

It's so funny how we can go without food or water for days, and we can hold our breath for minutes at a time, and yet we can't go without experiencing ourselves for a millisecond. There's no way of escaping our inner world. Information keeps rolling in, and rolling out. It's constantly being sensed, and felt, and observed, and assessed. It's endless.

33.

Now I'm thirsty and not for vodka. I might move toward the kitchen. Water helps everything, and I don't know why I forget to drink it. Apparently, we've already been dehydrated for like half an hour by the time we realize that we're thirsty. I'm not sure how information like that is meant to help a person. I mean, you can't know you're thirsty until you're thirsty.

When I was at boarding school a phys-ed teacher told us that it's best to sip water rather than skull it, because our bodies can only absorb 30ml at a time. I remember being really disturbed by this idea. I started obsessing over where the rest of it went. Surely the fluids that we drink go through this whole intricate process inside of our bodies before we wee them out? People aren't buckets. What we swallow must change form and find other uses. There's no such thing as "waste" really. What was she on about?

It's amazing how destructive the wrong information from

the right person can be. Like, when a doctor says "Take this," it's so easy not to ask "Why?" and to take it, and when the dude who sets up the TV says "Don't leave the screen on pause because it'll burn the plasma" it's so easy to say "Ok" and not "What is plasma?" and "How does it burn?" The same goes for "eating protein" and "dry cleaning" because, like, why? Cows live off grass, and what if I hand wash it in cold water?

Gosh, the kitchen in this house is adorable. The ceiling is high, and the wooden cabinets are worn around the handles, and everything is very well used, and loved, and the epicenter of everyone's day-to-day activities. They must spend a lot of time in here doing their dishes, and drinking wine, and laughing, and getting upset. Oh, they have a water filter, too! Rain down on me, sacred drops!

It's so lovely that no one who lives in this house owns it. We don't own the earth so why would we dream of "owning" a property on it? We're just visiting. Even if we buy land, it isn't ours. Not really. Renting is such a great reflection of our transient reality as human beings. I don't know why people get funny about it.

My ex-boyfriend's stepmother once said that the house he was renting was "good for a rental," implying that rentals weren't inherently "good." She shared this over dinner one night after insisting that she would buy him new crockery, as if it were this grand gesture and major contribution to his life. Like, somehow, her buying him new dishes would have been bettering whatever idea he had of himself, and of her.

The irony being that each of the plates she was scraping pasta off, and avoiding peas on, had been carefully selected from different thrift shops and vintage stores around the country. A story and an experience went with every single one. The crockery that guy had accumulated was more consciously chosen than anything she had ever chosen for herself in her entire life. So I guess it's understandable that she couldn't comprehend it.

There are dried hydrangeas hanging upside down from the wooden ceiling beams, and uneaten canapés on the counter, and the fridge is full of dips, and prosciutto wrapped in baking paper, and tomorrow's juice, and today's milk. Everyone seems to have their own shelf, too. Like, someone doesn't prioritize their physical well-being, because there's hardly anything on their shelf: a half-eaten jar of pickles, an old stick of butter still in the foil, a moldy jar of feta in oil with thyme and peppercorns. There's another person who might carry a bit of extra weight—physically, emotionally, mentally—because you can't even see the back of their shelf. It's so full. There's a carton of eggs, three jars of the exact same homemade relish, a large block of milk chocolate still in the paper, an opened can of kidney beans, a small wheel of Brie cheese in Glad Wrap, and a few unevenly stacked plastic containers with leftover meals in them. The third shelf—

"Hey, would you like some smoked salmon?"

"Oh. Ah, no, thank you."

"You seem very interested in the fridge?"

"I am."

"Not hungry?"

"Not really."

"That's chill, that's chill. I just can't shut up about the salmon because I smoked it, see? And I brought the capers, and the diced red onion, and the cream cheese, and the little bits of toasted fucking sourdough, and the little fucking dish over there. Yep. All me, baby. Sure you don't want a smidge?"

"I don't eat animals."

"Philosophical or health reasons?"

"What's the difference."

"Touché. So, who do you know?"

"At . . . this party?"

"Yeah."

"Umm. Someone who used to live here."

"Right? Well. I don't know anyone who lives here. I came with friends. Pretty sweet pad, though. I fucking love high ceilings. Where do you live?"

"Across town."

"Mysterious. That's chill, that's chill. I can dig it. I like your kimono."

"Thanks."

"And your fringe. There's something about chicks with fringes."

"Is there."

"Yeah."

"Hmm."

"Is that a martini you're sipping?"

"Umm. Yeah."

"Did you make it?"

"Yes."

"Care to . . . hook a brother up?"

"Ok."

"Maybe in a jar? Man, share house jar-glasses. What can you do?"

"A psychic once told me to never trust a man who smiles with his teeth."

"Lol! Really? Why? What are you supposed to smile with?"

"Your eyes."

"Do I not smile with my eyes?"

"No."

"You can't see my eyes from over there."

"Yes, I can."

"No, you can't. Shiittt! Strong fucking drink!"

"Too strong?"

"Nah, nah. It's good. It's good. So do you have a boyfriend lurking about somewhere, or?"

"Not really."

"Not *really*?"

"I think I might...leave now."

"Wait, wait, wait. Are we vibing, or?"

"I'm not sure."

"Stay a bit to find out?"

"I feel like I've...stayed."

"How about some coke?"

"Ah, no."

"K?"

"No."

"P?"

"No, thank you."

"They're cruelty fucking free."

"I... highly doubt that."

It's so hard to leave people wondering when their inclination is not to wonder about anything at all. Guys like that are only focused on penetrating the spaces that they occupy, because they're usually congratulated for how successfully they manage to do so.

He was outside the kitchen door talking with a group of people when I walked in, and it clearly didn't matter to him what I was thinking, or feeling, or what my attention was already on. He needed it, and he was willing to do almost anything to get it.

Everything he did and said seemed cute, and innocuous, and self-effacing, and hospitable, when it was actually an attempt to dominate me and our interaction. I'd bet that in almost any given social situation he wants to be seen as the funniest, and the sexiest, and the most considerate, and the most intelligent, and the most charismatic, and the most creative, and the most competent, and the most original, and every moment becomes about him accomplishing this at the expense of all else.

He believes that the world exists for him, and whenever he enters a room it must become about him. All natural conversation falters and all silences are quickly filled. His curiosity isn't genuine—it has an agenda. Every glance and every gesture are part of a larger scheme.

His calculated clothing choices aren't expressive. They're tokenistic, predetermined, and stifling. Every cowboy hat, high-heeled boot, set of grillz, tattoo, skateboard, zany dressing gown, pair of colored glasses, loud shirt, silk shirt, leather pants, vintage baseball cap, quartz crystal, and piece of peroxide hair is desirous of a specific outcome, because he's arrogant enough to think that he can control how others perceive him.

Man. Some seriously huge stars must have collided the moment when receiving positive reinforcement from others became such a big deal. How did it turn into something that people will literally ditch their friends for, and chase after? Being validated and appreciated is supposed to come as naturally to us as breathing.

Am I meant to feel sorry for him? Am I meant to be all like, oh, poor guy, he just didn't know how to go about interacting with me? Probably. It's just that I can't always take responsibility for other people's limitations because they're too lazy or too scared to do so. It's important that they give themselves the love that they need. I mean, I've got my own fucking loving to do.

At least I didn't smile too much like I used to. I used to smile like a moron through almost every social encounter I felt uncomfortable in, until I read somewhere that smiling when we don't want to, or when we're afraid, or feeling awkward, is a blatant sign of submission. On some primal level, people assume that we're vulnerable and easily manipulated because we're smiling too much.

So if I had smiled at him out of fear, he would've thought that he was "winning" and getting what he wanted out of me. And I, in turn, would have been misleading him.

I feel trapped behind my face.

34.

My body has taken me upstairs, and as I ascended I barely registered the surroundings. I've moved onto the balcony, and there are people crammed together, clutching their beers, and smoking their cigarettes, and frowning. I'm a bit over this party. I'm thinking of Porkchop and of the sandwich that I am going to make and eat, and I'm starting to wonder why I even came. I suppose I wanted to feel like I'm a part of something and I wanted to connect with other people. Two things I'm technically accomplishing. I'm pretty sure that feeling alone in a crowd is a shared experience.

That guy reminded me of this dude I once dated who fingered me until I bled. The whole time I was saying softer, softer, and he was like... "This is soft," and I laughed and was, like, "Oh! I'm sorry. Is this your vagina?" He didn't answer. Although, if he had, I'm pretty sure that the answer would've been:

Yes.

Because despite the fact I have more than twenty years of intimate, bodily, vaginal knowledge—which I have thoroughly enjoyed the process of acquiring and which I am more than happy to share the details of with others—most of the men who have come into contact with my body and/or vaginal region haven't wanted to know anything about it. Especially when the wisdom that I've had to share involves saying no to what they're doing or the way they're doing it.

The men that I've been involved with seem to have a strong desire to know how to "do" everything, including women and their vaginas. Yet, more often than not, they're unwilling to learn about how women and their vaginas like to be "done." They cannot accept that every vagina, and every woman, has vastly different preferences. No two people or bodies are the same, therefore no two vaginas are the same.

The earth has a multitude of mountains, and rivers, and flowers, and volcanoes, and oceans, and types of grass, and snow, and wind, and lightning, and rain, and thunder, and sun, and cloud, and sunsets, and sunrises, and no two lightning strikes, or sunsets, are ever repeated. Ever.

It's important to resist the urge to put things we can't comprehend into cages and to try to make them dance for us.

I get so tired of being a woman, because I can never seem to be "done" in the way that others want to "do" me. I just want to take my body off, hang it on a hook, and grab some air, because every stroke, whisper, request, poke, brush, smile, squeeze, lick, kiss, and breath can feel like a fight for territory.

I haven't truly made love to someone or something other than myself in such a long time. I worry that intimacy and tenderness are becoming impossible ideals, rather than lived experiences. Surviving on this planet right now seems to be more about figuring out how to withstand being violated and exploited than it is about cultivating fulfilling relationships with ourselves, and with others.

It's like we've lost touch with what true consent looks, feels, and sounds like, because we're so inundated with ideas and information that we never consented to receiving in the first place. Now, we're so preoccupied with all of these visions and fantasies of how our lives are supposed to be, and how our sexual experiences are supposed to be, and how our careers are supposed to be, and how our bodies are supposed to be, that we don't actually know who we are.

And unless we take the time to stop and consider that, and what we value, we're never going to know what we want, or how to say no to what we *don't* want.

It doesn't help that being overstimulated and distracted has become a social expectation. Cultivating self-knowledge isn't seen as essential, because we can't pop it on a CV, or take a photo of it, or impress our friends with it, or use it to get out of our next shift. We can't pierce our septums with it, or use it to fit into jeans, or offer it up to the gossip that we chop up and eat for breakfast, lunch, and dinner, so as to ensure that we're spared from the slaughter ourselves.

A girlfriend once told me I didn't "bitch" or "gossip" enough and it was a problem for her. She found it "annoying." She was pretty, and wealthy, and a model, and she didn't have time for this particular personality flaw of mine. It was a hurdle to our getting on smoothly. So, in order to appease her, I started cutting myself up and offering the pieces of my own problems, struggles, and limitations—and it was just as entertaining for her as highlighting or hacking at anyone else's. She fucking loved it. Because honoring the multidimensional and miraculous nature of who we are is a bit uneconomical, and a bit inefficient. It's tricky to sum that shit up in a forty-five-minute lunch break. It's faster, and cheaper, and easier, to just hate each other, the planet, and ourselves.

"Love the look, hun."

"Oh, thanks."

"You look familiar?"

"Really?"

"Yeah, do you know Sunny?"

"I don't think so."

"Or Em?"

"No."

"Emma K?"

"No."

"Hmm. Oh, I know! You remind me of my stepsister! Hey, doesn't she totally remind you of my stepsister?"

"Ha-ha! Yeah! Totally."

"Why?"

"She dresses all noughties and shit."

"Right."

"Who do you know here?"

"Not that many people."

"You're very pretty."

"Am I?"

"Yeah. Do you have a boyfriend? Or a girlfriend?"

"No."

"My partner actually saw you earlier and said she thought you were really pretty. We, like, rate people. And you got a very high score, little lady!"

"Thank you. I think."

"Do you like my coat? My girlfriend can't get enough of it, and I have this photographer friend who can't get enough of it, either. The whole see-through thing makes everyone go mental."

“I see.”

“Snap!”

“Yeah, I like it.”

“Me. Too. Hmm. Let’s get our picture taken! Oi! Get over here!”

“I’d rather not.”

“Oh? Sad face?”

“Yeah.”

“Why? Or, why not?”

“I just... like being in the moment.”

“We are in the moment!”

“Yeah, I just don’t really want it to be captured and shot at, if that’s ok.”

“LOL. Ok?”

“You called?”

“Nah, nah. False alarm. Your pretty little friend here wants to ‘stay in the moment’ with me rather than have her picture taken.”

“Oh.”

“Hmm.”

“Can I go now?”

“Yes, baby. You can go now.”

“Is that your girlfriend?”

“More like my long-suffering husband.”

“How long have you been together?”

“Just over two years. She’s actually my fiancée. When the law passed I popped the question. The wedding is in April.”

“That’s sweet.”

“You’re sweet.”

“Hmm.”

“Ever been with a woman?”

“Kind of.”

“That means no.”

“Ok, then. No.”

“I have to pee.”

“Ok.”

"See you later, maybe? On the dance floor?"

"Maybe."

"Merry Christmas, Pretty."

She just kissed me on the cheek, and I suspect that it would've been on the lips if I'd been more open to it, which I wasn't.

She was startling, and bright-eyed, and she had big breasts, which I love. Yet there was something about the see-through jacket that created an atmosphere where the only way I could make room for myself was to retreat from it. Plus, I began to feel responsible for the sanctity of her union with her partner. Probably because making out with her wouldn't have been the right choice for me.

I have a theory that being in an amazing relationship with someone can be very frightening, because then there's nowhere else to go. We're stuck with amazingness. So we create drama, and fantasize about other people, and draw dimwits to us that we'll inevitably want to run away from, and attract those who will inevitably want to run away from us, and constantly dream of leaving, and we turn the amazing person that we're with into a piece of shit, so as to give ourselves an excuse to run away from them when we get scared enough.

Because once we've committed to waking up and looking at the same person every morning, and to sharing our lives with them, and to being honest with them, we risk losing everything, every day. The stakes are much higher than if we're dating a whole bunch of people, or a few of them, or no one in particular.

When we're in a committed one-on-one relationship, we can't just bounce between whoever or whatever suits our agenda, or our ideas of ourselves, or the bite-sized chunks of intimacy that we can handle while juggling multiple partners.

Whenever I've had to coordinate with more than one partner, I've learned nothing except for how to devalue myself. My energy has become everyone else's. It was about texting this person, and organizing things with that person, and going to this appointment with the other one, and having an intervention with them about that, and considering something they said in a text, and how that relates to something the other person mentioned at coffee. I mean, I can barely *breathe* let alone think in an overcrowded space. So there's no way I'm ever going to thrive with multiple partners.

I also read somewhere that we're becoming more inclined toward one-on-one relationships as a species. In the beginning we were designed to propagate, yet now there's no need to. It's more important that we channel all of that creative and sexual energy into building sustainable and well-connected communities, not into giving birth to more of them.

There's no longer an evolutionary drive for more relationships, and more children, and more rogue semen, and more mess.

35.

Some guy just knocked into me and spilled his drink on my shoes, and I'm not even sure that he realized, and I can't even bear to look at him, because I can't even be bothered having to deal with that. You know. His face. Thankfully, my shoes are patent pleather, and the contents of his drink just casually dribbled off their surface and onto the balcony's well-worn wooden planks.

It's started to get pretty hectic up here, and I have a fear of foundations caving beneath me. I dream about it all of the time. It's become ridiculous. I literally wake up laughing when it happens now, and Porkchop gets the fright of his life over, and over, and over again.

I can see two guys sitting in a corner of the backyard downstairs in dark-green plastic chairs, and I feel compelled to go down and join them. They're lunging, and parlaying, and lunging, and parlaying, and looking around the party, and sipping their beers, and lunging, and parlaying. It reminds me of watching my father and his friends around the dinner table engaging in something I could never keep up with, between mouthfuls of Camembert, crusty baguette, red wine, and the occasional grape.

Dueling must be bonding for testosterone-driven creatures. My therapist once told me not to take people's attempts at "intellectual debate" and "casual chat" so seriously. Like, when someone asks "what I've been up to" or "what I think about that" or whether or not "I agree" with something, it's important to remember that it's "just about the back and forth," he said. "What you actually say is of less significance."

Which I interpreted to mean that it's best to treat "casual conversation" like a game of ping-pong, fencing, or tennis. It isn't about cultivating a deeper awareness of one another or learning anything. It's about "I haven't been up to much, what about you?" or "Absolutely right!" Or "No way, mate!"

So I'm going to go downstairs and over to those guys, and I'm going to sit down with them and see what happens.

"I don't think privilege even exists."

"What? How can you even say that? It's so embedded into our culture. It's everywhere! We are so much more privileged than everybody else. Especially in this country."

Oh, crap. I feel like I've just sat down in the middle of a court case, and I've swiftly been appointed judge, witness, jury, prosecutor, defense, and transcriptionist. They're both becoming more self-conscious. Their eyes and mouths are moving faster. My role here is important and yet I don't want to perform it. I want to rewind everything back to when I was up there on the balcony, deciding whether or not to come down here, and I want to choose a different path. A different door. A different box. The blue pill not the red one.

My solar plexus has started throbbing like it used to when I was alone in a room with my father, and he would raise a subject that I didn't want to discuss, because I knew it would inevitably lead to my holding him accountable for something he didn't want to be held accountable for.

Dad couldn't tell the difference between being blamed for something and being responsible for something. Every discussion was about one person being right and the other person being wrong. There was nothing else, and no in-between, and no other options. He didn't see himself as someone who was equally answerable for what unfolded in any given communication.

So if I came to a different conclusion about something, or if I requested that he change his behavior in some way, or if I asked him to explain something that he had done, which I didn't understand, it was always seen as an attack, and a ploy to persecute him. It was never simply a call for change, or a need for softness, or an evolution of the relationship that we had. It was never about learning or growth. It was war.

"How? What's an example of me being more privileged than anybody else? If anything, it's just the opposite. I feel like

I've been prejudiced against because of who I am. I've felt misunderstood. It's relative."

"Well, there's lots of different privileges. For one, you're less likely to be sexually harassed or raped. Every time a woman goes out she has to be thinking about how to stay safe. Do you know the statistics? They're out of control. I can almost guarantee that every woman you know has probably been harassed, bro."

"I don't think that's true. None of my ex-girlfriends have ever mentioned anything like that. And my sisters are so chill going out on their own and being independent. Like, maybe a small percentage of people have had problems. I just don't know anyone who has had those experiences."

"What do you think?"

"What do I think about what?"

"Do you feel like women are going through this all of the time?"

"Yes."

"So, what? Every time you go out, and every guy you speak to, you're worried that he might be a rapist?"

"Yes."

"What?"

"Every man I know has had the potential to be a rapist. And I've been raped, so."

"Well, fuck. Sorry. I still...just...can't reconcile that that's every woman's experience."

"Bro, the fact that you can't comprehend that shows the level of your privilege. Like, the fact that you don't know what other people are going through is the definition of being privileged."

"Well, no. That's the definition of being ignorant. Anyway. It's women's responsibility to talk about their experiences, then. It's not my fault that they're not sharing that kind of shit. Fuck, though. Ok. It's just that I'm not a creep. Sure, there are people out there who probably do some fucked-up shit. It's just that I'm being defined by them. Don't you think that that's unfair? Like, I've never raped anybody, or sexually assaulted anybody, and none of my friends are like that."

"I think it's healthy for you to be questioning your behavior, and having more open discussions with women about it all can only be positive. Because, you're right, your privilege isn't the problem. Being unaware of it and using it irresponsibly is. I wouldn't be so sure about your friends, either. If you're not in the room when they're fucking some chick, you can't really speak for them. I suspect that you'd be surprised. The nice guys who get on super well with all of their bros are usually the ones to be wary of, in my experience. I have to go to the bathroom now. It's been nice talking to you both. Merry Christmas."

"Merry Christmas."

"Yeah. Merry Christmas."

36.

I wonder where the fucking bathroom is. Going to the bathroom is always a bit of a thing in situations like this. My focus has to become spatial rather than social. I have to figure out where the toilet is based on the sense of the environment that I have so far, which requires a different part of my brain.

It's nice to have something tangible to work out, though. Now that I have to go to the bathroom, I can walk through the different rooms of the house with a sense of purpose. Whereas, when I haven't had to go to the bathroom, I've had to walk around pretending like I've got something tangible to do in order to *seem* purposeful.

Idleness, or appearing to be lost or alone, or like you're just reflecting upon something, isn't valued in social environments. Even standing still for a tad too long or just noticing the fact of existing is considered to be distinctly unproductive and antisocial. It implies that we haven't been chosen.

When we're busy, we've been chosen. Someone or something

wants our attention. Being in a state of oversaturation, or overwhelm, suggests that we have a tribe, and that we fit in, and that our attention is going toward something outside of us, and that we belong.

Focusing on our inner world has no social currency. I mean, no one is standing around waiting to congratulate us for stopping to feel how we feel, and to consider what we want, and to question why we choose to behave in certain ways. If anything, our doing this makes others uncomfortable.

However, I've noticed that when I treat my inner world as sacred, every interaction that I have with the outside world becomes sacred, too. How I treat myself is a reflection of how I treat the world and, in turn, how the world treats me.

Nevertheless, I make sure to adapt in social situations and to do everything I can to shift myself into a purposeful, energetic, outwardly oriented space, because I know it serves the neuroses of the people around me. It's important to acknowledge the process of adapting, too. Otherwise I'd have nothing of my own at all and I'd just become an adaptation. A mindless shadow following everyone else around.

So when I acknowledge the choice to adapt, I have consciously chosen a course of action and exercised my greatest power as a human being: choice. I am choosing this. I am choosing this. I don't have to choose this. I am choosing this.

37.

There's a sign on a door that says "bathroom," which is promising. Although, there's a massive fucking hole in it, and I can see the back of a girl dressed in black standing there, talking to someone who must be using the toilet. Nice. This could take a while. Even once I'm in there I'm going to have to be quick, because I don't want someone's entrance into my toilet time marking the end of it. I want to mark the end of my toilet time when I deem it appropriate to mark the end of my toilet time.

Ok, so a man has just approached where I'm standing and everything has slowed down. He's waiting for the bathroom, too, and I've become acutely aware of my face for some reason. The same thing happens when I'm getting a massage and they roll me onto my back and start working my arms, and hands, and the muscles around my mouth start tensing and flinching in a weird way and I can't stop them. There must be some ligament in my arm that attaches to my mouth or something.

The practitioners I see probably go away and write things in their diary when they can't remember my name, like, "Twitchy Face Girl on the 10th" or "Weirdo with the Face Works for Lymphatic Drainage on the 30th." That's what I would do. That's how I would remember me.

Anyway. The long, rectangular body before me is dressed in a very thoughtful way, and from what I can ascertain via conducting a few quick perfunctory glances is that his face has clarity and softness about it. The angle of his jaw, and cheekbones, and brow are square and defined. Yet his eyes, and skin, and facial hair, and lips, are less sure of themselves. They're more unruly, and ready to be tested. He's like a Viking who figured out which direction to take across the ocean in order to discover a new land, while everyone else was running around, and raiding, and stealing materials to build huts, and hacking off their neighbors' heads with ice picks.

His mouth keeps tightening as if he might burst into flames or cascade into laughter. Our bodies can't contain whatever this is. We're both struggling to keep the sparkles inside, which is a magnificent sign during a first meeting.

He's holding a beer, and there's a sweater draped and tied around his shoulders in the way that I imagine the Kennedys would have draped and tied sweaters around their shoulders when they were throwing parties and watching polo in the Hamptons.

All of a sudden, I'm really glad I didn't go with the chopsticks in my hair. It's a miraculous thing that those chopsticks are very far away from where I am right now. I have a feeling that people with sweaters draped and tied around their shoulders don't necessarily warm to those wearing kitchen utensils as hair accessories.

I just took a deep breath and saw a bright-pink web tracing its way from my heart and vagina to his heart and penis. It's strong and effervescent. The mere idea of it is making me blush. I want to weep, and fall to my knees, and whisper to the universe how grateful I am for being here, and for feeling what I feel, and seeing what I see, and knowing what I know.

The toilet door just flew open and three girls came bumbling out, each grappling with various states of explosiveness in relation to one another. They're adorned in spangly black things, like spiders, and I don't think that they meant to dress identically. That just happened. How terrifying.

"After you."

"Thanks, umm. There's a massive hole in the door."

"Oh?"

"Yeah. Would you . . . be able to stand in front of it for me?"

"Sure."

"I won't be long. I don't think. I mean, I won't be. I just . . . Yeah."

"I'm cool to stand here. No worries."

"Thanks."

Now I don't want to take too long and I also don't want to *not* take too long, because either option would potentially conjure unhygienic and/or poo-related themes, which I don't want to do. One time I made a diarrhea joke within days of meeting a guy, and he said "Too far" before ceasing all contact with me.

Then again, one of my more long-term boyfriends insisted that I keep the bathroom door open when I shit because he liked how my thighs looked sitting on the toilet.

So I need to figure out some sort of middle ground between these distinctly paradoxical experiences to ensure that the timing of my use of the bathroom is utter perfection, without too many sound effects or foibles.

Perhaps a wee, a straightening up, a dab more perfume, a lippy top-up, and, oh yeah, flushing and washing my hands and whatever. Although, there's no hand towel. I wish I'd realized that before getting carried away washing my hands with the very refreshing designer liquid soap that's been provided. Mmm. Mandarin. Now the doorknob is going to be wet when he touches it. Yuck. Oh, fuck it. I'll wipe it with my kimono! Ok.

"All yours."

"Would you do me the honor?"

"Of course."

"Thanks."

Oh, wow. I love being asked for help. Now I'm guarding the door for him. I feel so proud. I can't even hear what's happening in the bathroom. He definitely wouldn't have been able to hear the intricate and well-crafted sound show that I put on.

"Done."

"Cool."

"It smelled good in there. I think it was your perfume. Did you . . . top it up?"

"Yeah, I did. Would you like some?"

"Ah. Ok. Sure?"

"Here."

"I've never seen anyone put perfume behind their ears?"

"My nana always told me to dab perfume behind my ears so that when I walked past people, they'd get a whiff."

"And why a dab on top of the head?"

"It's for the pineal gland, and it feels good. I don't know."

"Thanks."

"My pleasure."

"Sorry about before."

"Before?"

"On . . . the balcony."

"Oh?"

"I spilled my drink on you."

"Oh!"

"And then you sort of . . . disappeared."

"Right."

"Yeah."

"Did you follow me down here?"

"No. I mean, I don't know? Sort of. Maybe. I had to go to the bathroom. Then I saw you standing outside of the bathroom and I thought that that might be a good opportunity to own up. Then I saw that your shoes were, like, plastic, and I didn't feel so bad, and then I didn't know what to say, and then the whole bathroom door thing happened, and . . ."

"A lot happened."

"It did."

"Yeah."

"Do you . . . need a drink top-up?"

"Sure. That'd be nice."

"Cool."

"I can imagine that . . . you do, too?"

"Yes. Yes, I do."

"Great."

"I think I'm following you?"

"Ok."

"Would you like a beer?"

"Not really. I could make us martinis?"

"Martinis?"

"Yeah."

"Ok?"

"I left my supplies in the kitchen."

"I'll follow you."

38.

Sometimes I worry that I'm completely out of my depth in the presence of a man. This one seems to be keen to go where I lead, which is nice. I'm not being rushed. Nothing is being forced. I can feel butterflies in my stomach. Warning signs gently reminding me to stay sensitive and awake. There have been too many times in my life when I have heard myself justifying the bad behavior of a man, because I seem to be addicted to enabling it, and then I become stuck in loops of escaping, and being trapped again, and deluding myself into thinking that that's what I want.

"Damn."

"What?"

"Someone's taken them."

"Where did you leave them?"

"In a bag just here."

"Yeah. Leaving vodka out at a party is, like, an invitation."

"Right."

"Was it expensive?"

"What would be expensive?"

"Like, was it a good brand of vodka?"

"Yes."

"That sucks."

"I think I know who took it."

"Who?"

"The smoked-salmon guy."

"I don't know him."

"Probably for the best."

"Do you want one of my beers?"

“Where are they?”

“Follow me.”

“Upstairs? You’re keeping your beers upstairs?”

“It’s the Wild West, baby. Trust no one.”

39.

"Whose room is this?"

"No idea."

"I wonder why they like pictures of houses and driveways in Palm Springs so much?"

"What's not to love? They're inoffensive. There's a sky, a vintage car."

"They just seem so . . . soulless."

"I think that's why people like them."

The room we're in is so large and yet the person who lives in it has chosen to remain so small. I wonder which shelf in the fridge is theirs. Probably the empty one. Their bed is a futon, and there are no bedside tables, or books. The walls are white, and the bed sheets are white, and their clothes are hanging on a silver rack. They wear a lot of black. There's a set of white wooden drawers, and a retro lamp sitting on the floor. There's no desk, although I can see a laptop poking out from under the bed. There's a mirror resting against one of the walls, along with some framed photographs. I read somewhere that having artwork on the floor is really bad feng shui.

I bet they have a room somewhere else filled with all of their shit, and mess, and stuff, and crap, and all of their favorite little bits of nothing, and whatever morsels of a history and a personality that they might have had once upon a time.

I once dated this guy for a couple of months who had a super-minimal room, just like this one, except he also had these really calculated, pigeonhole-shelf things, and a really slick sound system built into the corners, and all of these little skull sculptures. I remember thinking, "Wow, this guy has absolutely no baggage."

Then I went to the bathroom in the middle of the night and I accidentally—well, I don't believe in accidents—walked into this other room, which, I swear, could have been a hoarder's. It was astonishing. There were books, and pieces of paper, and old clothes, and technology, and crap everywhere. Soccer boots and dirty socks. I remember the dirty socks really vividly. They were white, with thick red stripes around the top, and the whole room smelled like compost. I didn't know what to say to him about it the next day so I pretended as though I hadn't seen it.

"Here."

"No, thanks."

"You don't want a beer?"

"No."

"This room is really depressing."

"I know."

"Maybe they're a tourist or something."

"In their own life?"

"Pretty much."

"Do we go?"

"Yeah, ok."

We just received so many interested and suspicious looks leaving that bedroom. One of the only reasons I can get through parties is by convincing myself that everyone's too busy focusing on themselves to notice me and what I'm up to. Yet here we are, blatantly being noticed at every turn.

"Do you know many of these people?"

"Not really. I came with a mate I think I lost a while back. He was trying to pick up this girl. Anyway. It's probably best we parted ways. You know. Give him some room to do his thing."

"Right."

"So did you want a drink of any kind?"

"Maybe I'll just get a water."

"I'll get you one."

"Ok, thanks."

"Where will you be?"

"Outside."

It's so strange to be presented with someone that meets a need I didn't even know I had. I'm always looking to connect with other human beings, and when it actually happens I'm always surprised. I wonder if I'll see him again. I have a feeling that I'm going to and I'm nervous about it. I want to be very conscious of this moment, and appreciative of it. I want to breathe it in, rather than scare it off through being neglectful, or insensitive to its presence. I want every shooting star I've never seen to know that this glimmer of hope hasn't passed me by.

I don't want to overstate it, though. I don't want to crush it by obsessing over it. I don't want to tamper with it. No moment tampering! I just want to see it clearly. Whatever I am, whatever you are, whatever this is. Help me see it clearly.

"I get scared when I look at the stars."

"Really? Oh, you put lemon in it. Thanks."

"No worries."

"Why?"

"They make me feel small."

"Hmm."

"Have you ever seen a shooting star?"

"Heaps of them."

"Oh, no. You're one of those people."

"What people?"

"Those people that shit just... magically 'happens' to."

"Have you ever seen a shooting star?"

"I've seen, one, maybe?"

"Do you look much?"

"Probably not that much!"

"I look every night. So. That'd make my odds better."

"I'd say so."

"I've seen a UFO, too."

"Really?"

"Mmmhmm. Although I don't tell many people about it."

"And."

"What?"

"Are you going to tell me about it?"

"Would you like to know about it?"

"Yes."

"Well. I was at the beach and I couldn't sleep. It was 2:30 in the morning and I went outside and sat on the balcony in my dressing gown. I listened to the ocean and I cried. I was thinking about my dad, and looking up at the sky, and this enormous bright orange-and-purple light shot in all different directions at this incredible speed, not that far above the horizon line. It was like a comet, except it went like this, and then like this, and then it just disappeared. It came out of nowhere, and quickly disappeared back into nowhere. And I just knew. I felt connected to something bigger than my own brain. It was . . . reassuring."

"Shit."

"Yeah."

"Have you, like, looked it up?"

"Looked what up?"

"If other people have seen the same thing?"

"No. Never."

"Well, my shooting star sighting, which I can barely remember, seems pretty insignificant now!"

"No, no, don't do that. It has whatever meaning you want to give to it."

"I was in the middle of a breakup when I saw it."

"Right."

"Yeah. I went outside to have a smoke because of course I was still smoking. I've been off cigarettes for a couple of years now. Anyway. Back then I was still smoking, and I would use going for a cigarette as an excuse to get away. I feel bad about that. Although, she did all sorts of shit to get away from me, so. Whatever. We'd gone to the Blue Mountains in an attempt to salvage our relationship, and, of course, it wasn't salvageable. We fought the entire time. Then I went outside, looked up, and there it was."

"Was it a sign?"

"Of what."

"I don't know. Something?"

"Something, maybe."

"Cool."

"Yeah, it was."

"Who's that?"

"Who?"

"There's a girl over there that keeps looking at you."

"What does she look like?"

"She's got a pixie cut."

"What's that?"

"Like, really, really short hair."

"Maybe make it a bit less obvious that you're sussing her out?"

"Am I being obvious?"

"I don't know. Yeah. I just..."

"Ok, well, it's not safe for you to look yet. Her body language is, like, very open in this direction. I think that she really wants an opening with you. It might be a while before she—oh, ok, go now!"

"Oh. Yeah, I know her. Sort of. Her hair is shorter than it used to be. I worked with her."

"She definitely has feelings for you."

"What? How could you possibly know that?"

"I just... know."

"How?"

"She wants to connect with you, and I'm blocking her path. It's bothering her. I just... know."

"She has a boyfriend."

"That doesn't matter."

"Yes, it does."

"Oh, of course it matters. It just doesn't matter to *her*. She mustn't be very content. Like, her having a boyfriend isn't stopping her from trying to seek out your attention."

"I don't want to look again, so I'll just take your word for it."

"Ok. Did my sharing this upset you?"

"No. I don't know. Maybe."

"Ok."

"Is she bothering you?"

"Um, no. It's just something that I noticed. Her gaze keeps landing upon you whenever there's an opening for it to do so. Like, when you were walking toward me with the drinks, and when you sat down, she did this double take. Then she looked me up and down, before realizing that I could see her looking me up and down, and then she looked away again. That doesn't really answer your question, though. Um. Does it bother me? Well, if I weren't allowed to talk about it, it would bother me. If I felt like I had to pretend like it wasn't happening, it would bother me. The fact that it's happening in and of itself doesn't necessarily bother me, so much as if I had to lie about it or something."

"Do you want to move?"

"Oh, I don't mind."

"I'm feeling pretty uncomfortable."

"Because of what I said, or . . . ?"

"I don't know. Maybe."

"Ok."

"Maybe we can move when I've finished this beer?"

"Sure."

His body language has become really closed off and tense and twisty, and his legs and arms are crossed, and it's a strain for him to make eye contact with me now. Damn. I seem to be addicted to identifying and expressing what I see, and I'm now remembering how I read in this book one time that it's very important not to disguise brutality underneath a demeanor of frankness and honesty. Maybe I need to be gentler. People think that seeing is blaming. They assume that through articulating what's happening that they're being judged, and ridiculed, when they're actually just being seen. I don't mean to condemn. A scientist doesn't judge the organisms in a petri dish. Scientific experiments aren't about making the organisms right or wrong for doing what they're doing. It's about watching how they work, and getting to know how they behave and interact.

And I've noticed that people become slaves to what they don't want to see, so I've become obsessed with making sure that they see everything. I'm terrified of being deceived and of becoming delusional, because I've so often been deceived and deluded.

My parents lived and breathed lies. They mistook them for intimacy. Whenever I'd tell the truth, or say what I was seeing, they'd tell me that I was being too sensitive, or too much, or too melodramatic. Then I would doubt myself and what I had seen, and I'd become deluded, after having been deceived. Because, in truth, what I observed was always happening. Like, *always.*

So I'm not going to ask him about his feelings for that girl, even though I really want to know, because he hasn't talked about them, and I can sense that there's a lot of unresolved shit going on.

It's just that I also read somewhere that it's very important to go slowly and calmly with men. They process things at a different speed. Especially relational and emotional things. One book even said to wait six to ten seconds after asking them a question before saying anything else. 1, 2, 3, 4, 5, 6—

"So what's with the kimono?"

"What do you mean 'what's with it'?"

"Why are you wearing it?"

"It was my mum's."

"I like this bit."

"The roses? Yeah, me too."

"Did you go to a costume party before this, or . . . ?"

"No. Are you talking about my kimono in this way because of what I said about that girl?"

"Why?"

"There's, like, a tone."

"Oh, fuck. Probably. Sorry. Yeah. Umm. I hardly know her. My ex-girlfriend always sensed that something was up with her, too, and I never listened. I actually gave her—my ex, that is—a really hard time about it. So, you know. It's pretty weird you said what you said."

"Right."

"It's one of those things, you know? Ships in the night."

"Oh, ok."

"I'm really happy to be sitting with you, though."

"Ok."

"You're really beautiful."

"Ok... Thank you."

"You're... unusual."

"Am I?"

"Yeah."

"Well. I'm glad we got your blatant need to gloss over awkward things with niceties out of the way."

"Ha. Right."

"What star sign are you?"

"Why?"

"Why not?"

"Guess."

"Give me a second. I need to sense your energy."

"Ok."

"Virgo?"

"No."

"Aquarius?"

"No."

"Leo?"

"Yep."

"Ooh."

"Ooh."

"A natural-born leader."

"Hmm."

"You look a bit like a lion."

"Yeah."

"It explains the signet ring."

"What?"

"It's a lion, right?"

"Oh, yeah. It's my family's."

"Do you know much about your star sign?"

"Just that I'm a Leo."

"Well, you must get your natal chart done."

"My what?"

"A natal chart. You go to an astrologer, and they tell you where all of the planets were and what they were up to when you were born. Different alignments mean different things. I love it."

"I sense that."

"Once I was talking with my dad about astrology and he was like, 'Look, darling. I like to keep two feet on the ground.' And I was like, yeah, well, the ground is on the earth, which is a planet, that's part of a galaxy, which is in a universe, that's a tiny fraction of the cosmos, and he said nothing. It's just that we're so deeply affected by the sun, and by the moon. I don't see how all of the other planets could just be . . . ornamental."

"I see what he means."

"Really?"

"Yeah. He just wants to focus on what's in front of him. Not what's out of his control."

"Hmm."

40.

He keeps sweeping this bit of hair back from his face, and as he does his signet ring glistens. His hands are so angular and large. They must make things. Although he's definitely not a tradesman. He has very artistic, very delicate, very long, very visionary fingers. They don't have a firm grasp on the world. It's as if his soul was a bit unsure about whether or not it wanted to be here. I wonder if he was a cesarean baby, like me. My head was riding up Mum's spine during the labor, so they knocked her out, and Dad freaked out before they tore me out.

His eyes are emerald green. Or maybe they're hazel? They change. He's very intense up close. More intense than at first glance. There are deep lines across his forehead when he raises his eyebrows, and more subtle ones around his mouth. If he spent a lot of time in the sun I don't think he'd burn. I wonder what his ancestry is? Lion insignia could be associated with England, or Ethiopia, or Sweden, or Jerusalem.

"My mum wears kimonos."

"Really?"

"Yep. Not, like, out, though."

"I like the sound of your mum."

"Yeah, she's great. She's . . . really great."

"What are her kimonos like? What colors are they?"

"Maybe green or red."

"Maybe green or red?"

"I'm color blind, so."

"Oh."

"Yeah, I struggle with red and green mainly."

"Right. This one is red."

"Yeah, I probably would've guessed that."

"Hmm."

"So. Anyway. What d'you do?"

"As in . . . what are my gifts and how am I using them to serve the world?"

"Sure."

"Well, it's a constant process of unfoldment."

"I can imagine."

"Right now, I'm spending a lot of time with myself because I'm drawn to doing that."

"So... you're not working?"

"I am. Just not in the traditional sense. It's not like I clock on, and clock off, and have a salary, and a manager, and a lunch break for an allotted amount of time, five days a week."

"So definitely not working then."

"No. I guess not."

"That's... privileged."

"Is it?"

"Yep."

"How?"

"You must be loaded. Like, your family must be supporting you or something. Or you're on welfare. Or you must have savings."

"Or maybe it's just my divine right to do nothing when I'm called to do nothing, because it's my world, too, you know?"

“You got an inheritance or something, didn’t you?”

“Yes.”

“The universe ‘provided.’”

“In a way. In other ways, it didn’t.”

“I see.”

“What about you. What are your gifts and how are they serving the world?”

“I’m working as a draftsman at this architecture firm in the city. I’ve been there for too long.”

“Why?”

“I’m tired of working for other people. I want to design what I want to design, you know? I might just get another beer. Do you want another water?”

“Ok? Thanks.”

“Or maybe we can move on? Do you want to sit somewhere else, or . . . ?”

“Ok, so, the topic of work just completely spun you out.”

“What? No, it didn’t. I’m just . . . thirsty.”

“Right.”

"I'll just go get that beer and be right back."

"Ok."

We must have been sitting on these cement steps in between these two pot plants for a while now. One of the pots is holding a struggling fern, and the other is filled with dirt, and cigarette butts, and a half-drunk bottle of beer. A breeze has just rolled in, although it's still pretty steamy. The storm mustn't be too far off. I wonder how close we are to the lunar eclipse. I have no idea what time it is, and I can't see the moon. I haven't seen it all night. The house has emptied out a bit, and that girl has moved on. They're playing acoustic music.

I might reapply my lipstick. I can't actually see my face or lips, so I'm going to go by feel and allow the mental effort that that requires to calm and center me. There. I might fluff my hair with my hands, too. When I was younger, I was obsessed with fluffing my hair with my hands, and the girls at school nicknamed me Fluffy.

I'm going to stretch my shoulders and roll my neck around. No cracks, which is good. I read somewhere that bones cracking indicates dryness and rigidity in the body. So let's channel the feeling of being fluid and supple. Yes, all of my muscles are juicy filet mignons and my bones are light, and strong, and melodic, like wind chimes. I'm redoing the positioning of my legs and I've pulled the spandex skirt down a touch. My legs are sticky. I've rolled my ankles around, and, we're back.

“That was a big sigh.”

“Was it?”

“Something troubling you?”

“No. Just . . . existing.”

“Difficult?”

“No, I’m just . . . aware of it.”

“And it didn’t, by the way.”

“What didn’t? Do what?”

“When you asked me about work. It didn’t spin me out. Or maybe it did. I was thinking about it the entire time as I was going to get the beer and I talked myself into this place where I was pretty sure that it had had no effect on me. Although, now, saying it out loud, I’m pretty sure that it did.”

“Right.”

“In fact, I’m certain.”

“Why?”

“It’s a long story.”

“My favorite.”

"So I studied architecture after school. I didn't get into Melbourne University so I went to Sydney. It was a huge deal. A massive move. Blah, blah, blah. I met a girl pretty quickly and that helped. We lived in a share house together. We were going through a lot of the same shit. I don't think I could've gotten as far as I did without her. I quit a couple of years in. Getting an architecture degree, and your master's on top of that takes, like, five years. More, even. She continued and I didn't. I came back to Melbourne. We broke up. That was, like, three or four years ago. Since then I've been here, working under this guy in the city. Everyone tells me that I'm lucky to even have this position given I didn't finish uni.

"My ex is now working for this huge architecture firm in Sydney. She's one of the only people in our year that got in. I'm not sure how to say this diplomatically... basically, accomplishment was like a drug for her. It's why I loved her, I guess. She got off on the status that came with 'making her way up' or whatever. So when I bailed on the course, you know. Our being together didn't add up anymore.

"There was also this other super-hungry and high-achieving guy in the course who was constantly vying for her attention. He'd oi me out in front her, and in front of our friends, and during class, and in the fucking hallways before lectures. I almost fucking killed him once. I went to punch him and then pretended like I was joking. Seriously, though. I could've fucking killed him. Anyway. She seemed to empathize with me, and she hated on him, too, and we'd talk about what a douche he was.

"Then I heard that they were together and it fucking sucked. I mean, I don't care. It's just sad how predictable people are. They end up right where they start. I thought she'd kind of grow out of her obsession with hierarchy, and status. Like, once she progressed further along, she'd just want to express herself. I don't know."

"Is that what you want? To express yourself?"

"Definitely. Although I'm the guy who's 'lucky' to be working under this fucking top-bun of an architect. He literally wears a top bun. I'm prone to them, on occasion, too. Usually when I'm exercising. It's just that wearing a top bun is that guy's fucking *religion*. He's the younger brother of one of my mates. He did this epic presentation project thing in his final year at Melbourne, which got picked up by some law firm in the city and became their foyer. He got all of this media attention and interest from investors. So he started his own firm. Sorry, studio. Collective. Whatever. I don't even know what it is. He's two years younger than me. He's all right. It's just that people who receive copious amounts of validation freak me out.

"I'm the guy who had to move back in with his parents when he couldn't handle shit. It was a fucking disaster. I fucking hated living with them again. I was in such a bad state. While I was trying to find a position in an architecture firm somewhere—with all of my zero credentials—I started working at this café. Man. I don't know how people do it. I started going out with a girl who worked there. She was one of those people who's super-content working in the service industry. She loved it and would just save, and go traveling, and save, and go traveling. She didn't want anything more. She was, like, the total opposite of Sarah. My ex-girlfriend in Sydney.

"She was really into drugs, too. Traveling and drugs. They were the extent of her aspirations, and it was a relief for a while. Then it became a dead end. I put on so much fucking weight. Oh, man. It was the worst. I just ate and worked at this café and got rejection letters on a daily basis. I smoked like a chimney.

"My parents would look at me every morning and be like: Ahh, eggs this morning, mate? Bit of a sit-down and a chat, mate? And I'd be like, gah, NO DAD! I was fifteen again. I started to wonder why I had left Sydney. It just didn't feel right, you know? I could never meet the criteria. I felt trapped. It seemed so at odds with what I knew to be the reality of working in the industry, you know? Not that I knew. I could just sense that it wouldn't help beyond giving me a piece of paper. It seemed like such a waste of time. I can't believe the lengths people go to for fucking pieces of paper."

"So what do you do working for top-bun?"

"He's really into redo's for cafés and bars, which is super–de rigueur. Lots of painted bricks and communal tables. I think he wants to work on art galleries eventually. He occasionally gets private jobs. Like, private houses. They're good money. Not that he needs it. I'm always doing the drawings for him.

Technically, I'm a draftsman not an architect. Although, I like doing shit by hand. I'm an old-fashioned guy. I can do designs in my head. I don't need to draw stuff up. I get a feel for things and I can piece them together. That's not on-trend, though. And it's definitely not what they're lecturing down at Melbourne Uni. Oh, no. You've gotta have all those pieces of paper flying about down at Melbourne Uni.

"The irony being that this guy, top-bun, is such a cretin. He studies the design sensibilities of other cultures and brings them here and knows how to make them appear is if they were, like, his own divine inspiration. He's a good businessman, I guess. It's just ironic that he sees himself moving into the art world: the crux of innovation and originality. Which he, certainly, is not.

"I don't know. I just get tired of drawing up shit that he ultimately doesn't want to be doing. He's so over bars and cafés, and yet he keeps taking them on because he likes the street cred that they give him. It's hard working for someone who wishes that something else was happening for him. He's nice and he appreciates what I do. I've made suggestions outside of what he's gotten me to draw up and he's always incorporated them. It just doesn't feel right. I need to go out on my own to do what I want to do, and there's no way that's going to happen."

"Why not?"

"Capital."

“Oh. So. If you could have your way what would you be working on?”

“Houses. I’d like to work on communal-housing projects. I’m really into figuring out environmentally friendly ways of constructing something that allows for lots of natural light, and privacy, and heaps of garden, and vegetation. In, like, unexpected places. Also, like, structures that are relatively inexpensive to construct and economic in terms of their use of materials. Umm. You know those apartment blocks with courtyards in the middle? They’re kind of sprinkled throughout the city, and in Europe? This city totally needs more of those. Or at least the suburbs do. They create this combination of harmony, and community, and quiet that really appeals to me. The world needs more of that. Especially the world’s cities. The only problem is that cities are all about upward mobility, and building higher, on less. So, yeah. I’m interested in how people can live, and rest, and work, and operate harmoniously and environmentally. How they can feel safe, and held, while living in a densely populated area. There’s this architect in New Zealand who really homes in on that. I love his work. Top-bun has zero interest, though. So. I’m not exactly serving the world with my gifts. I’m serving fucking... top-bun.”

“You’re just accumulating knowledge.”

“Maybe. There’s just so much responsibility in starting something up. I don’t know if I can be fucked.”

“There’s a lot of responsibility serving top-bun, too.”

"True."

"I have a belief that we, like, choose our problems. When I'm considering a challenge, or a change, it's usually on the back of wanting new problems. Maybe when you reach the point of wanting new problems, you'll be ready."

"Hmm."

"You drank that beer pretty quickly."

"I did."

41.

Moving on from here seems logical, although I don't know how to go about it. I'm not sure what I want or what direction I want to go in. A therapist once told me that when it comes to communicating with men, when I'm not sure what to say, to say nothing. I really liked the idea of this. It seemed so logical. However, there have been occasions where I've taken what she said so literally that it's become dangerous, and absurd. Like, I've heard myself accepting that a man just needs to yell at me, and at life, in order to process his feelings, because apparently men struggle in the expressing-feelings-and-being-vulnerable department, and as a woman choosing to be in a relationship with a man, it must then be my responsibility to take him, and his inherently violent and egotistical nature, on.

I must be still, and silent, and know god whenever he's hollering, and writhing, and pacing the well-worked neural pathway from anger to brutality and back again, over, and over, because he knows nothing else, and he isn't about to stop, or learn how to change, without my help.

So rather than stating what I want directly, or doing what I want, when I want, I shall say very little, and go to the gym regularly, and meditate when stuck in traffic, and gather my thoughts before walking through the front door, and cry in the bathtub, because if I didn't—and if I said and did what I wanted without restraint—the man in my life wouldn't be able to comprehend it.

Because I'm supposed to be shy yet chatty, needy yet reserved, bitchy yet unassuming, emotional yet quiet, and, above all, the best at everything, across the board, at all times, always. And I'm supposed to have complete, sovereign, autonomous rule over my life. Because I do, and I am partly responsible for this. All of it. The silences, and the inertia, and the resentment, and the drama—and I must live with that.

Besides. I don't want to overload a guy with my capacity for clarity and detachment because when I'm not around I can't even expect him to clearly state that, let alone act like, he's the co-creator of a sacred space with me. He's not going to know the power or the value of that until he has destroyed it, which is a process that I'm inevitably going to have to live through, and be patient with, because I love him dearly, and frighteningly, and unconditionally, and fuck my life godfuckingdammit.

I love being loved by a man. I want to wake up, and look into the eyes of my chosen captor, and hug him throughout the day, and care for him as I would myself, no matter how much it hurts, because if I can do that—and if he and I can rise to the task of the healing that is called for through our union—surely, we can save the world.

So I relish in being his sweet, delicate, porcelain little buttercup, right up until I'm his fleshy, naughty, juicy, fierce and succulent little sugar tit because, yes, it is one or the other, and it takes a lot of work for a guy to appreciate that the woman in front of him is all of these things, and more, and that there's an infinite number of experiences to be had in the relationship that he has with her.

Nevertheless, I worry that by choosing to ride the waves of this process with one man, I must ride it with all men. The world that we live in can't seem to handle my picking and choosing the attention that I receive, or who I receive it from. Communications between the sexes would become too complex and too unpredictable for the Neanderthals and philistines among us. So I must pray on a daily basis that my heart and my body are kept safe, despite the odds, and through it all, always.

Oh. An intense urge for physical contact just washed over me like a hot flush. My cheeks are burning. Although not enough for him to notice I don't think. I'm looking at the arch of his shoulders, and the way that they curve around and slope into his arms and around into his hands like a rainbow. I want them wrapped around me. I want to be squeezed, and I want to stop thinking and talking.

I want to put my forehead against his and to shut my eyes. I want to smell his neck and underarms. I want to sense their heat and their wet pulsating against my nose and face. I want to feel the consistency of his skin in different places: where it's soft, where it's coarse, where it's rough, where it's taut, where it's hairy, and vein-y, and bony, and muscly, and smooth, and hard. I like his thumb. I want it in my mouth. It's a hitchhiker's thumb. It's bent, and quite elegant. I want it running all over me, up and down, up and down. Then I want my stomach against his stomach and I want to breathe him in, before feeling the weight of him, and falling asleep, and then waking up.

"So. What now?"

"I don't know."

"My mate must have left ages ago."

"Do you live together? Or do you still live with your parents?"

"No, thank fuck. I don't live with him and I don't live with my parents. I love him, I just couldn't live with him. I'm in a share house with this couple. They're super-chill. We have totally different schedules. What about you?"

"I've been living in the same place for a while. On my own."

"Really?"

"Yep. With Porkchop."

"Porkchop."

"He's a cat. A ginger cat."

"Whereabouts?"

"Toorak."

"You're alone in... Toorak?"

"Yes."

"Come on."

"What?"

"That's pretty unusual."

"Is it?"

"Are you in a unit?"

"No."

"Townhouse?"

"No."

"Fuck me."

"What?"

"A girl living on her own in a house in... Toorak?"

"A woman. With a cat."

"A woman with a cat. Sorry."

"So?"

"It's like the wealthiest suburb in the city. Except from, I don't know. Albert Park, maybe?"

"Which suburb did you grow up in? Wait, let me guess."

"Ok."

"Armadale?"

"Close. Malvern."

"See. Your roots aren't that far from where mine are."

"How did you end up in Toorak?"

"Life, the universe."

"Right. What're you doing for Christmas?"

"The usual."

"What's that? Family?"

"Yeah. Just... at home. You?"

“I’m visiting my parents for the night. Although, I might drive home after lunch if I can be bothered. I dunno. I usually help Mum with some of the cooking on Christmas Eve. So. I’ll be doing that tomorrow.”

“What does she cook?”

“Everything. I’ve always wanted her to get everyone to bring a plate and she always refuses. She orders whole salmons, and scallops, and crabs, and makes all of these epic salads and, of course, her famous guacamole.”

“I love guacamole.”

“Who doesn’t. Hers is epic. It has chili, and garlic, and coriander, and red onion, and salt, and pepper, and lemon. I basically stay the night to get my fill of that fucking guac.”

“Hmm.”

“Hmm.”

“So do you feel like going for a walk or something?”

“A walk.”

“Yeah? It’s a nice night.”

“It is. Ok.”

“I’ll just go take a leak. You’ll be here?”

"I'll be here."

"Sweet."

"Hey?"

"What?"

"Oh, nothing."

"What!"

"It's ok! I'll be right back."

42.

I don't quite know how I'm going to manage this. High-heeled shoes are a blockade between me and my life. I hope he doesn't mind my going barefoot for our walk.

So-called women's fashion is completely orientated around restriction and restructuring. It's all very flattering, and fashionable, and desirable, right up until it isn't, which is usually around the time when we want to dance, or lie down, or inhale deeply, or make love, or take a shit, or eat something. I'm not surprised that so many women are drawn to pantsuits, and hoodies, and stretchy exercise gear, and "boyfriend jeans," and "tees," because it's either that or being tied up.

I'm pretty sure I wore this outfit tonight because I wanted to seem more approachable and non-threatening. By subscribing to some of the tropes of uncomfortable fashion, I am better able to blend in. It's like camouflage. Or at least that's how I justify it to myself.

A friend of mine who always become inflamed after eating

wheat, and dairy, and sugar once went to an addiction workshop where they were serving scones with jam, and cream, and fresh black coffee at the breaks. She thought, "Well, I'm here, and I want to fit in, and seem approachable," so she decided to eat a scone with the lot. As she did, a woman came up to her and complimented her skin, and asked about what she did to care for it, and how it had become so dewy. The irony being that her skin's dewiness was due in large part to not eating scones with jam and cream on a regular basis.

However, my friend might have seemed more inaccessible and unrelatable if she had been eating, say, one of her usual seaweed snacks that she'd brought from home, and sipping a chamomile tea with oat milk out of a thermos—and that woman probably wouldn't have approached her.

So, my wearing lipstick, and high heels, and spandex indicates a desire to belong and to connect. It says, "Hey, I don't feel entirely good about myself and I don't mind looking a bit silly and being in a bit of pain in order to be accepted; maybe we can be friends."

One year I went to the Melbourne Cup with a group of girls from school, and I didn't know how to dress comfortably and fit in at the same time. I wanted to bond through the gambling and through studying the form guide, and they all wanted to bond through preparing for the day rather than any of the activities occurring on the day itself. It was all about planning the outfits, and makeup, and practicing walking in high heels, and pitching in to pay for copious amounts of champagne and canapés.

Anxiety and physical discomfort were the main event. They were treated as inherent aspects of the occasion, and of the lead-up to the occasion. I mean, of course we were going to be hobbling, and drunk, and undernourished. Of course, we were going to get fake tans, and tailor-made fascinators, and shove chicken filets into our bras, and stick double-sided tape along the edges of our garments, and buy strappy stilettos in the hopes of a sunny day, and hard soil, which, of course, you never, ever get at the Melbourne Cup.

The cruelty that's inflicted upon the racehorses didn't get a mention in the lead-up, either. I didn't expect it. A multi-million-dollar horse broke its leg halfway through one of the races and was killed behind a vanity screen right there on the track where it had fallen. Apparently, the moment was cut out of the telecast and not one commentator mentioned it as the race continued to stream live to the nation.

Years later I reflected on the experience with a boyfriend as we were driving somewhere, and I wondered what I would choose to wear if I were ever forced to go again, and he said, "You women, you're all the same. It's all about what you're going to wear," and then he put his hand on my leg and went, "It's ok, I won't judge you. I'll support you if you want to go to the races and do all of the girly things."

I asked him to pull the car over. I undid my seatbelt and turned to face him. He kept his hands on the wheel, and the car running. I said, "No, that's not what I'm saying. And that's not what you say to me. I hear that you want to care for and support me. However, if you're truly going to do that, that is not what you say. You say that you cherish who I am, and the person that I have become, and the extent of the struggles that I've been through in relation to my gender, and to my body, and to my womanhood, and to the community. You say that you support me in participating or not participating in these strange, barbaric, cult-y rituals, which I have become susceptible to in the past, because I have wanted to belong at the expense of my sanity, and well-being. You say that you appreciate the level of detachment I've been able to cultivate in relation to something so contentious, and cruel, given the pain I clearly carry around inclusion, and exclusion, and having friends. You say that you're proud of me, and of who I am, and of the person that I've become, and am becoming. You say that you honor me, and all of the choices that I make, and am going to make. Then you emphasize that you're incredibly proud to be with a woman who thinks, and feels, and explores things to such great depths, and with such discernment and compassion."

He laughed, squeezed my thigh, and growled.

43.

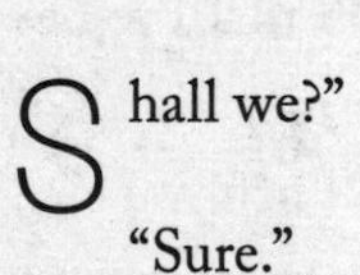

hall we?”

“Sure.”

“Is there anyone you need to say good-bye to?”

“No.”

“Me neither, I don’t think. Which way?”

“Left?”

“Sure. Can you smell that?”

“Jasmine.”

“Yeah. It feels like it’s going to rain.”

"I know, I've been hoping for that all day."

"Hmm."

"I'm going to take my shoes off."

"I was wondering how you'd go in those?"

"Not so good."

"Yeah."

"Can you see a bin anywhere?"

"I'll keep an eye out."

"Thanks."

"There's a possum!"

"It looks like a baby."

"I never get over seeing those. The bats are pretty freaky, though."

"Melbourne is Transylvania."

"Yeah."

"It's so quiet."

"I've almost gotten used to the haze."

"I know. It's amazing how readily we can adapt to . . . tragedy."

"Hmm."

"Can you see the moon?"

"No. There's a bin."

"Great."

"Wait, what? You're throwing those out?"

"I've had enough."

"Ok?"

"It's nice to feel the ground. Oh, my arches. Just give me a second."

"Are you going to be ok barefoot?"

"Are you going to be ok with me being barefoot?"

"Not really."

"Why not?"

"Glass, shit, sticks, rocks, piss, shards. Fucking syringes. I don't know."

"It's just that I'd rather be free at this point, you know?"

"Not really."

"We can keep going now."

"There's a cat."

"Oh, what a cutie."

"You don't often see white cats."

"No."

"What do they mean? Or symbolize? Or whatever?"

"Death, probably."

"What?"

"Or wealth, maybe. I can't remember."

"Here, puss, puss. Its eyes are different colors, too, I think?"

"Yeah."

"I'm not mad on cats."

"Why not?"

"They're too picky. Dogs are more... unconditional."

"Right."

"What?"

"You know what."

"What!"

"You're a Leo."

"Hmm. Why do you love cats so much?"

"I don't 'love cats.' I live with a cat that I love. If I met a dog whose soul journey happily coincided with mine, then that would be synchronistic, and destined, and perfect, and I would be open to that. However, until then, I'm a woman who lives with a cat. Nothing more, nothing less."

"Her name is 'Ceridwen.'"

"It's keh-rihd-wehn. The C is more like a K: it's Celtic. Ceridwen is the goddess of, like, rebirth and fertility and transformation. She's the goddess of the white moon."

"Right."

"Sorry. I just corrected your pronunciation."

"That's ok. Does doing that come from your parents?"

"I don't know?"

"It definitely does."

"Whatever."

"That must be tough."

"What would you know about the toughness of that?"

"One of my best mates in high school's parents were always correcting him when he spoke. His dad was in the family business and his mum was an academic. They'd correct Max and his sister's grammar over the dinner table. She barely spoke, surprise, surprise. They even corrected me one time when I was over there.

"They also had this really intense need to be greeted all of the time. It was always, hi, Dad! Kiss, hug. Hi, Mum! Kiss, hug. Bye, Dad! Kiss, hug. Bye, Mum! Kiss, hug. There was even a running commentary while we were in the house: Just going to watch TV, Dad! Just going out into the garden, Mum! It was exhausting.

"One time we didn't say hello to his dad when we got back to the house after school, and we just ran up to Max's room because we were laughing about something, or rushing, I don't know, and his dad came in five minutes later and goes, 'Max. May I have a word with you? In... *the study*?' The study was his dad's private space and it was totally off-limits. Max only ever went in there when 'having a word' was called for. I could hear his dad yelling at him through the wall. 'Who do you think you are, mate? Whose house do you think that this is? You too good to say hello to your old man now?' I felt so embarrassed for him. We never talked about it. His parents seemed so loving in so many ways. They had art all over the house, and cars, and they played tennis. They were always having interesting people around. There were heaps of books, and his mum made these spelt muffins every day. Then we just turned into really different people. I think he designs skate gear now. So, yeah. If you had to go through anything like that, it must have sucked."

"I don't know. I also don't know any different."

"True."

"She really likes you."

"Yeah."

"Off she goes."

"Bye, Ceridwen!"

"Her work here is done."

"Yeah. Oh, there's some courtyard housing. You know, apparently, the reason why this style of architecture died out is because of cars. An apartment block with parking spaces at the bottom became more of a priority. Like, more of a priority than nature and space just for the sake of nature and space."

"That's so depressing. Nature and space are so important. It's amazing to think that it can . . . lose its value."

"I know. People see cars as more valuable now. The next style of apartment block that came into fashion was literally called the dingbat."

"No?"

"Yeah. We'll probably see one or ten of those. They've got garages at the bottom."

"Ok."

"Which way do we go now?"

"Straight."

"You know this area pretty well?"

"No. I just feel like going this way."

"Ok."

"Do you live on the north side now?"

"Yeah."

"Do you like it?"

"Yeah. I associate the south side with my parents and with high school. So. Compared to that, the northside is amazing."

"Why are you still living in Melbourne?"

"No idea, really. I traveled a bit, with Chloe. That girl from the café. We went to South America and Southeast Asia. I also went to the US with my family when I was a teenager to visit relatives. One time I went skiing in New Zealand with a friend and his extended family, and it was beautiful. Intense, though. It was with his entire family at their lodge-cabin-thing. I haven't been to Europe, so. Who knows? What about you? Why are you still here?"

"It's just...where I am."

"Yeah."

"I'd love to go to Egypt. I just don't want to fly anywhere. I don't like flying."

"Fair enough."

"Hmm."

"Hmm. I think I can hear a fountain?"

"Yeah, over there."

"Hmm. I haven't seen many Christmas decorations?"

"No."

"A lot of these houses are very on display, though. The fences are so low. I like higher fences."

"You're more into privacy, and... sacred space?"

"Yeah."

"You might like my house, then."

"Really?"

"Yeah. It's pretty... enclosed."

"Right. High fence?"

"Yep. And a big garden."

"Cool."

"Hmm."

Oops. I didn't mean for that to sound like an invitation. I was merely stating a fact. Damn! There's always an expectation that we aren't actually saying what we mean. Like, ever. It's assumed that our true intentions are hidden behind all of these curves, and blurs, and lies, and deceptions, and other people are supposed to do all of the workings out. So when we actually say something, it's presumed that we aren't actually saying it, and that we must be saying something else.

Now he probably thinks I was insinuating that we go back to my house. I mean, I'm not opposed to that, I just hadn't planned to waltz into it so soon. He wouldn't make the same mistake. The way he talks is very considered and clear. He wouldn't stretch an inch too far from exactly what he wants to express. I'm not surprised that he's had heaps of social experiences, and school friends, and girlfriends, and run-ins with large families, and trips to the snow.

People would underestimate him and want to have him around. They'd think, "Oh, he's a loyal friend and we haven't seen him for a while, what's he up to?" As distinct from, "Yes, well, that one was trouble" or "Oh. How is he doing? Getting on ok?" People would always think that he was doing "fine" even when he wasn't. He exudes a very potent sense of responsibility and agency.

He's quite contained, and he doesn't share too much about what's going on for him in the moment. It's as if he doesn't want to be exposed or to go too far into areas that he hasn't already thought about. Like, he won't go into the unknown in front of me. He wants to absorb what's happening and then go away and assess things for himself before coming to any kind of conclusion about them.

"There's the moon."

"Shit."

"Hmm."

"Eerie."

"What time is it? Has the eclipse happened?"

"We don't get to see the eclipse."

"What?"

"Only the Northern Hemisphere gets to see this one."

"Really?"

"Yeah."

"Damn."

44.

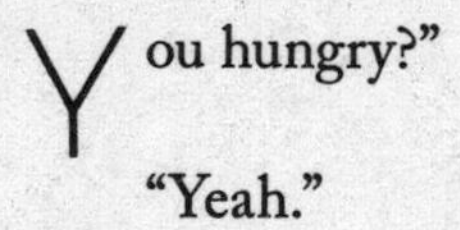

You hungry?"

"Yeah."

"What do we do?"

"Umm. Would you like to come to my house for supper?"

"Supper?"

"Yeah. I was going to make myself a sandwich."

"Ok."

"I don't want to have sex."

"Ok."

"I just...want a sandwich."

“Ok. Umm. What kind of sandwich?”

“Well. I’ve got wholemeal sourdough, and almond cheese, and red onion. I thought that I’d rub some garlic on the bread, and butter it before toasting it with the cheese and red onion, and then I’d put in the avocado and the lettuce at the end. Maybe add some sauerkraut or coriander.”

“Yum. Do you have Vegemite?”

“Of course.”

“Ok.”

“Ok?”

“Count me in.”

“Ok.”

“Yeah.”

“I guess we need to find a cab?”

“There’s a main road up there. Do you want to be carried for a bit?”

“The spandex situation makes that a bit difficult.”

“Everything you’re wearing makes things a bit difficult.”

“Yeah.”

"So?"

"What?"

"Do you want to be carried, or?"

"Ok. Yes. Thank you. I want to be carried."

"How's that?"

"Good. Yeah. Fine."

"It feels like you're slipping. The silk makes it feel like you're slipping. I keep having to hoist you up."

"Do you want to put me down?"

"Do you want to be put down?"

"No."

"Ok."

"You sound a bit stressed?"

"I'm not stressed."

"Ok. You smell good."

"Do I?"

"Yeah. Like . . . man. Damp hair, and. Man."

"Not exactly the crisp, aftershave-y vibes I was going for."

"Sorry."

"I'll hail a cab."

"Ok."

"There's more going the other way?"

"Nah."

"Ah . . . Yah?"

"Hey! Yo! Over here!"

"Hey, man, we're going to Toorak."

"Sure thing, boss."

45.

The skin on the back and sides of his neck was so cool and soft against the grain of his polo T-shirt. He's a lot stronger than I thought he would be. Yeah, Germaine Greer would laugh hard at that one. Oh, the unexpectedly strong love interest! It's true, though. He's not bulky or anything. He just fully inhabits his body, which is unusual. He lives at the edges of himself during a time when a lot of people are very disconnected from their physical bodies.

Most people don't feel alive when you touch them. Their handshakes and air kisses are either too tentative, or too forceful. Their minds are constantly racing ahead of whatever they're doing physically. And yet their bodies have safe and unsafe zones, which you need to be mindful of when you're embracing or touching them in any way.

There are certain areas of the body that people would rather not think about and other areas that they don't want you to see. Like, a gentle touch on the upper arm might not be noticed by some people. Yet for others, it would be totally invasive. I've known women who don't like their upper arms being seen or touched at all. Ever. They carry a particular energy around that part of their body, and when it's touched it triggers waves of anxiety and tension and self-consciousness.

I wonder where his sensitive zones are or if he has any.

Every guy that I've ever dated or been in a relationship with has been at war with his body. One dude had epic digestive issues and they'd always flare up right when it was my turn to speak. During our very short-lived relationship he checked himself into the hospital for a week, and I visited him every day. I remember sitting and laughing, and when he asked me why, I told him how ironic it was that hospital environments were the antithesis to healing environments.

I mean, you can't get a proper night's sleep because you're being interrupted around the clock. The beds are uncomfortable. It smells like disinfectant. The windows don't open. There's some old guy coughing and spluttering next to you. The ceilings are low. It's difficult to access sunshine. It's impossible to find nutritious food. There are no masseurs or acupuncturists.

He was quite taken aback when I said this, because he had checked himself into the hospital in order to heal and to get steroid injections to calm his stomach or something. All of his joints were puffy, and he was red in the face, and hobbling to the toilet every half hour or so. Like, by choice.

Nevertheless, he tried to impress me with stories about how he was still working hard and doing everything that his workmates expected him to do. He was "keeping up" while lying there in the friggin' asylum. I could sense that he wanted a hearty congratulations for this. He seriously thought that conducting meetings with an IV drip in his arm while wearing a hospital gown was admirable and noble. Everyone else was telling him he was an inspiration. They were saying how amazing it was that he was able to work and stay "active."

I looked down at my shoes sitting on the rubber floor before I gently tried to explain that I didn't view this as a triumph. The fact that he was ignoring his body and doing everything that he could to medicate it and override its messages was not impressive to me. The idea that he was using this time to fill his mind with distractions and to please others was mortifying.

I said that if he were able to rest and to move with his body's unique waves of energy—and to come to understand its gentle language—he might feel better. He might actually learn something about himself and his existence. It was even possible that what he once viewed as debilitating could become something that gave him stronger access to who he was, and what he truly wanted, and what he had to offer the world.

He was very angry with me about this, which was fine. We all get angry and frustrated. It's how we express our anger and frustration that counts. He broke up with me, and I smacked a pillow against a wall, and yelled, and cried, until I got over it.

46.

Where does he need to turn?"

"Umm, go right at the next traffic lights, then left, and then left again. It's not too far down after that."

"I feel excited."

"Do you?"

"Yeah. This is quite an adventure."

"Hmm. Just here, on the right. Anywhere is good."

"$13.50."

"I'll get it! Sorry, I was . . ."

"Thanks. Goodnight!"

"Night!"

"What're you doing?"

"I just have to find the remote for the gate."

"You leave the remote for the gate in the bushes . . . next to the gate?"

"Yeah."

"Your fence is more like a wall."

"I know."

"A fortress."

"Yah."

"How big is this? Like, the whole block?"

"I think so. I mean. Yes."

"How big is the block?"

"Come in."

"Oh my . . ."

"Hmm."

"Umm. So. Ok. You live here with your parents?"

"No. Not really."

"Right. So. Where are your parents? At the beach house or the villa in Spain or...?"

"They're dead. Technically... they're dead."

"Oh... I'm so sorry. I just... I'm... I've always known that places like this existed in Toorak. And I expected something unexpected, I just... I don't know."

"Ok."

"What's that?"

"An altar."

"I've never seen such enormous crystals before! Are they even crystals? Or geodes? Is that what they're called?"

"Yeah."

"Can I have a look?"

"Of course."

"Wow."

"Hmm."

"Is that... Heath Ledger?"

"Yeah."

"I love the stone frame."

"Thank you."

"Did you build this?"

"I had it put together."

"Is it ok if I walk around it?"

"Of course. Take your time."

He's not touching anything or interfering in any way with the altar, which is very different from my previous boyfriends and dates. They've all wanted to touch the altar, and take photos of it, and borrow bits of it, and use it as a backdrop for little vids that they're making, and content that they're creating. They'd ask me where I got it, and where the idea of it came from, and how much it cost, and how I had done it, and why I did it, and then they'd try to copy it at home, or would use images of it without crediting its origins.

It's interesting how someone so sensitive to physical spaces and their design might be more inclined to treat the world and its structures with more tenderness and respect. I don't think that that's very common.

I went to Hanging Rock a couple of years ago under the false assumption that I could have a quiet picnic there, just the rock and me. I didn't want to have a soy cappuccino at a café, or navigate hordes of people, or go fishing, or see a concert, or buy memorabilia, or take pictures, or even look at a map.

However, as I approached that gnarled fist of a former volcano—known as Ngannelong to its traditional custodians—I became aware that I had to pay for a parking spot next to it. And in order to have a picnic near it, and to walk around it, I had to pay for a ticket. The rock had opening hours and it was closing soon.

It was an amusement park. The only way to develop a relationship with it was to pay for the privilege of enjoying it, because a group of people had decided that it was theirs, and they wanted to make money out of it. So not only did I have to pay them, I had to abide by their rules of engagement with it.

They'd even stuck signs up about what they claimed to be the rock's history and a few paragraphs about the tribes that guarded and occupied it. They said that they wanted to "pay their respects," and I wondered how exactly "respect" was being paid in the way that "business" was being run on the rock. True respect requires more than lip service and an entry fee. True respect requires communication, and creativity, and the integration of values that at first seem foreign, which then gain meaning as we come to understand and appreciate them.

It's never been fashionable to include or consult with Aboriginal Australians, which has been a great loss for everybody. I've always been curious about how they'd go about preventing bushfires. Not that every single Aboriginal person living in Australia right now would have ideas about that. It's just that their ancestors must have known a thing or two about how to interact with the bush, and with the sun, and with the wind, and with the plants, and with the weather patterns.

Yet for some reason their knowledge isn't taken seriously. There isn't even a representative for Aboriginal or Torres Strait Islander people in Parliament. There are more of them dying in custody than there are holding office and positions of power and responsibility. Although there have been a zillion commissions, and reviews, and inquiries into the importance of including and consulting with them—and governments around the world have condemned Australia for not doing so—it is still seen as an act of charity or pity, as distinct from something that would be beneficial for everyone.

And as a result of this oversight, their lives are shorter, and their suicide rates are higher, and they have lower socioeconomic outcomes, which creates fewer opportunities. Plus, we don't get to develop a relationship with them, and with the land that we live, work, breathe, eat, die, and make love upon.

I read the other day that Australian law only recognizes native land if a continuous cultural connection to it can be proven. So, not only have Aboriginal people been dispossessed of what was theirs to guard and care for, we've then told them that they have to prove they were dispossessed of it before we'll give them restricted access to it, because we're scared of them doing to us what we did to them.

And fair enough. I don't know what I would do if someone arrived at my gate tomorrow and claimed that this land was theirs now. What unspeakable horror. This is my home. What would become of my altar, and my bathtub, and my books, and Porkchop, and all of my plants, and all of the pictures of my family? Where would I go to feel safe and at peace? What would happen to my children and my children's children? Where would they live? Would they ever have a sense of who they were, or where they came from?

Probably not. That knowledge would be replaced with the horror of what happened on that fateful day when the land beneath their mother's, or grandmother's, or great-grandmother's, or great-great-grandmother's feet was taken from her. That moment of disrespect and betrayal would live on in their genes, and in their DNA, and it would come to define them more than their roots and their history. It would live on in their bones, and in their memories, and it would haunt them, and those who stole from them, until reparations were made.

"I can smell those roses from here."

"Yeah."

"May I sit in the hammock?"

"Of course."

"Wow."

"Hmm."

"What a place."

"Yeah."

"What happened?"

"To . . . my parents?"

"Yeah."

"They died in a plane crash."

"Oh."

"Hmm."

"I'm so sorry. How old were you?"

"Seventeen."

"Shit."

"They traveled a lot."

"Right."

"They died doing something they loved, so. I don't know. They were at their best when they were traveling together."

"Did you ever go with them?"

"Not really."

"Shit."

"Yeah."

"It's really beautiful here."

"Thanks."

"Do you leave the front door open?"

"Yep. No one's getting over that fence, mate."

"No."

"And Porkchop likes to come in and out. So if you hear a little Christmas bell, you know who it is."

"Ok."

"Is it spitting?"

"I think so."

"You know, if you sit under that tree over there when it's raining, like, full pelt, you won't feel a drop. The leaves are so thick."

"I like that you put a seat around the trunk of it. Is it a Moreton Bay fig?"

"Yeah. My grandfather put that seat there. He used to sit outside and paint watercolors. He loved it here."

"Was this his property?"

"Yeah. He had heaps of siblings and his parents, and his parents' parents, owned real estate around the country. Mainly in Western Australia. They were miners, and developers. They bought up heaps of land in the 1800s and then over the next couple of hundred years big industrial companies rented it, or bought it, or developed farms on it.

"Dad's dad was the only one of the siblings who was drawn to the Big Smoke. He loved Melbourne. He was an artist at heart and he adored being so close to the galleries, and to the theaters, and everything. His favorite place to eat was Pellegrini's on Bourke Street. He liked the feeling of being in Europe without actually having to be in Europe.

"He always sat in the kitchen area of the restaurant out the back. They'd make up a special dish for him: mushroom risotto with this truffle oil that they kept in a special cupboard or something. He'd have that, and a glass of white wine. He had friends in Parliament and they'd occasionally dine with him. I have a feeling that he might have been attracted to men. I'm not sure. It's just a feeling. Anyway. He bought this property and cared for it before passing it onto Dad. And Dad was an only child, like me. So. He lived here, and now I do."

"Where's your extended family?"

"In different places."

"Do you ever see them?"

"Not really."

"Not even for Christmas?"

"No. They're fine. I tried to do a couple of Christmases with them in Perth. I just can't stand the sense of loss when they look at me. A person can only take so much pity, you know? Actually, it's not even that. It just doesn't feel like Christmas with them. Christmas for me is . . . being here."

"Right."

"Hmm."

"I can imagine that a lot of planning and consideration goes into this garden. It's still got a mind of its own, though. I really like that it's plant centric rather than landscaping centric. So many of the properties I work on are the opposite."

"Can I show you something?"

"Sure."

"Do you have any coins?"

"Ah, no. I don't, like, carry loose change."

"That doesn't matter. Follow me."

"Is there a bore water system?"

"Yeah. And three rainwater tanks."

"Cool."

"Oh, wow! Thunder!"

"Very dramatic."

"Yeah. Ok. Here she is."

"Whoa."

"Meet Aphrodite of Ephesus. She's based on the fountain at Villa d'Este, in Italy. My parents went there for their anniversary one year and when they came back they had her built."

"Oh my god."

"Yeah."

"Or, oh my goddess, I should say."

"Yes."

"She looks so... fertile."

"I know."

"Hmm."

"Make a wish."

"Ok."

"Choose wisely. It'll come true. She's very powerful."

"Ok."

"Don't tell me what it is."

"Ok."

"Wow, the moon."

"Cool."

"Done?"

"Done."

"Follow me."

"Is this the same path that we took to get to the fountain?"

"No."

"Oh. Ok."

47.

I'm not sure how to go about introducing him to the house. I feel a strong desire to talk a lot and to explain everything, kind of like a tour guide. I also want to quickly run up to my room, and put all of my shit away, and make sure that all of the toilets are flushed, and that my bed is made, and that the most fragrant candles are lit, and that the best chandeliers are dimmed, and that doors to all of the rooms that I don't want him to go into are shut. Yet I can't control his experience of me. No matter how many sinks I clean, or lights I turn off, or eclectic pieces of furniture I attempt to elucidate the history of, his experience of me shall remain his.

One time I went to MONA (Museum of Old and New Art) in Hobart, Tasmania. Forty percent of all the convicts that were sent to Australia were sent there, and, I swear, the rolling hills and dense, dark-green forests still hold their unsettled energy. Aboriginal Tasmanians are known as Palawa, and, up until recently, they were wrongly thought to have died out.

Everywhere I went, and everyone I saw, or met, seemed to be in on some secret. I'd look up at houses, and blinds would abruptly shut or lights would turn off. Every night I dreamed of people in hoods traipsing underground walkways, and knocking in code, and tattooing each other in blood.

The day I was going to MONA it was raining heavily, and I asked for an umbrella at the reception desk of my motel, and, without blinking, the woman with acrylic nails looked at me and said, "Sorry, love. We dun 'ave any a'those 'ere. You'll just 'ave ta... make do." I went outside, stood in the rain, looked back, and saw her watching me.

Soaked, I took the MR-II ferry to the gallery. The attendants at the entrance—who were dressed in black from head to toe—handed me a headset, which was supposed to be my virtual tour guide. It was going to talk me through all of the pieces and installations across the gallery's multiple levels. My parents had been to MONA many years prior to this and they'd talked about how amazing the virtual-tour-guide headsets were. Like, it was a main attraction for them. "There're such interesting stories behind each of the pieces!" they'd said.

I looked around at the other members of the public swarming the foyer and traversing the various spaces, ascending upward into the ether, all dutifully plugged into their complimentary devices, brows furrowed, moving quickly and purposefully.

There were families and friends and couples. I'd never been to a gallery with so many attendees first thing in the morning in the middle of the week. I subsequently learned that the gallery's owner, David Walsh, allows Tasmanians to visit the gallery for free.

So I paid the admission fees and walked a few tentative steps, headset in hand, before abruptly turning around and running straight back to the attendants. "I want to do it naked," I said, without meeting their gazes.

Then I walked through the carefully designed spaces, and absorbed each of the artworks, and felt my feelings, and thought my thoughts. I saw waterfalls, and tombs, and mirrored hallways, and neon lights, and darkened corners. I watched a mechanical intestine digest food. It stank. I waited in a queue. I got lost. I didn't know any of the artists' names, or any of the pieces' histories or narratives. I had an experience, not a lesson.

And I don't want to teach him about me, I want him to experience me.

"I'd like to invite you to take your shoes off at the door for sensory reasons, as distinct from cleanliness reasons, if you want. You don't have to, though."

"What do you mean by 'sensory reasons'?"

"I like how the marble feels underfoot. It's cooling and grounding. Someone once told me that in Japan they treat home like bed, and that's why they take their shoes off at the door because they're, like, getting into bed. Not because they're worried about dirt being dragged in or whatever. I don't care about that so much. Anyway, do whatever you want."

down and... he appeared."

"

."

n. He's a bit unsure about you."

ur fat phobia."

ike my jumper, though."

ke that as a compliment. He's just assert-
tatus."

ct that."

"Your Christmas tree looks red."

"Yeah."

"It's glowing."

"Hmm."

"There are so many presents?"

"Yeah. I . . . accumulate them throu

"Right. Like . . . For yourself?"

"Yeah."

"Cool."

"Thanks."

"Do you open them on Christmas m

"Of course."

"Is that your parents?"

"That's my favorite photo of them. They'
Rose Festival in Morocco."

"Wow."

"Mum loved roses."

"You're very different from her."

"I know."

"The shape of your face is kind of like your dad's, maybe?"

"Maybe."

"And he's looking pretty suave in that linen suit with the cigarette in his hand and everything!"

"Hmm."

"What did you do while they were away?"

"I'd spend time with my nana. Or a friend from school would stay. I don't know."

"Right."

"I might just take this spandex off."

"You've taken off an item of clothing at every location."

"Oh, that's better."

"Porkchop is following us."

"We're going into the kitchen now, so. Yeah."

"Right."

"Hmm."

"Do you have people over for dinner often? Or for parties?"

"Not really."

"It's so set up for that."

"My parents entertained a lot. Dad would create a menu and buy nibbles from the Prahran market. Olives, and breadsticks, and eggplant dip, and potato crisps, and dolmades. He and Mum would carefully select the group of people, and get all stressed out and tense, and inevitably it'd rain when they wanted to barbecue. People would sit over there and then move into the dining room and then into the lounge for, like, dessert and cognac. Socializing is such a circus."

"You keep the place so clean and tidy, though? Every house that I've been to that's this clean is either a display home, or the people living in it are motivated to keep it clean because people might come over or 'drop by' any second."

"Yuck. Droppers-by freak me out. Cleaning is a sacred rite. Do you clean?"

"Umm . . . sure."

"Lol."

"Ha."

"Can I ask you a favor?"

"Sure."

"Could you cut this for me? I don't like cutting bread."

"Definitely."

"I mean, I obviously cut bread for myself, like, all the time. I just . . . it'd be nice if you did it."

"Sure."

Oh, a moment just happened. I mean, lots of moments are happening. It's just that I experienced such a powerful charge in our electromagnetic field as I gave him the bread knife. It's amazing what asking for help can create. I didn't intend for that to happen. It just emerged like electricity. *Zing!*

I always seem to have something in my hand when moments like that occur. It's like if I'm too focused on them happening, or too busy desperately trying to make them happen, or feverishly anticipating them happening, there's no space for them to actually happen. I have to be in the middle of doing something else and feeling detached and then . . . there they are.

I stopped breathing for a second, and I read somewhere that shortness of breath or holding our breath stops the flow of sexual energy. So I'm going to keep breathing. Sexual energy is just a wave in the ocean between us. No need to flail about. Breathe. Breathe.

His belt brushed against my hip, and now I have a desire to rub myself all over him. I'm just going to quietly light the menorah with the shamash. We haven't kissed, or even held each other except for when he carried me. Do I say something? No, no. Of course I don't fucking say something! How absurd.

The energy field that we create together is so full, and intimate. People must obsess over the physical act of sex when whatever *this* is, is lacking. It's like sex becomes the outlet when we don't feel connected to each other emotionally and energetically.

I can also imagine how people would become completely fixated on sex if they were spending their days in jobs that they didn't want to be doing, and in relationships that they didn't want to be honest in. Sex would be a way of escaping, under the guise of meeting a need for comfort and closeness. Then the mere idea of sex, and of its release, would somehow make all other problems disappear for a minute—like a drug.

I mean, my body wants sex. There are definitely vibrations and pulsations rippling across my nipples and clitoris, and goose bumps are rising on my arms and legs at random, and I want to lick and bite my lips to self-soothe.

"Is he allowed to be up on the counter?"

"Ah, yeah. It's his counter."

"He's staring at me."

"You're new at the counter."

"True."

"He seems pretty chilled out, though. He's stopped pacing, and when he sits still like that, and just watches, he's holding space. He's guarding us."

"Guarding you."

"Probably."

"You don't toast it with the avocado in it?"

"No, no. I put that in after. With the lettuce."

"Good idea."

"Yeah. Just a schmear of Vegemite?"

"Just a schmear. Wow, your sandwich press is amazing."

"It was my nana's."

"I love the shell shape."

"Yeah. It's French. It does waffles, too."

"Do the handles get hot?"

"No."

"And are these all right sliced like this?"

"Yep."

"Is there anything else I can help with?"

"No, just sit. The press is heating up. Did you want some juice?"

"Yeah, thanks. In here?"

"No, the next one. In the door."

"Cool—and the glasses? Sorry."

"That's ok, in there."

"Oh, I could make you an alcoholic drink if you want?"

"No, no. Juice is good."

"So, like, how have you... survived?"

"Umm."

"I'm just... in awe. I think."

"Oh."

"Yeah."

"I don't know. Grief is pretty trippy."

"Yeah."

"Yeah."

"Is your nana still alive?"

“No. She died four years ago. Transitioned. Whatever.”

“Shit.”

“Hmm.”

“The house is so . . . quiet.”

“Yeah.”

“Does it unnerve you?”

“Sometimes.”

“That’s starting to smell pretty fucking good, isn’t it, Porkchop? I think I’m growing on him, don’t you think? He’s moved closer to me on the counter.”

“Maybe. Oh, look at him. I always find it so funny being in the midst of a really intense conversation or in the throes of some really intense thoughts or feelings, and then I just look over and see . . . a cat. Like, this creature that is just blatantly witnessing me and my experiences. He has no shame or judgment. He just watches. I love it.”

“Yeah.”

“Do you live with pets?”

“No. My parents have always had heaps of dogs, though. They have two now. Fred and Ginger. They’re poodles.”

“Oh, I love poodles.”

“Yeah.”

“Are they big?”

“Yeah. Big, dark, and curly haired.”

“Like you.”

“I guess.”

“They must miss you.”

“My parents?”

“Since you moved out.”

“I’m just across town.”

“Yeah. Umm. It’s not about physical distance.”

“Hmm.”

“Maybe it’d be nice to eat our sandwiches in the library?”

“The library. Sure.”

“It’s just down that hallway. Second door on the left. I’ll meet you in there.”

“Ok.”

48.

I always feel very self-conscious at this point in preparing a meal for someone. Like, when I'm finally assembling it all and plating it up. Most of the cooking process occurs without me having to think, and then I get to here, and I find myself questioning everything, and feeling pressure, and doubt, and second-guessing all of the steps I've taken, and hoping that it comes together in the way I imagined.

I don't follow recipes. I see them as propositions not rules. This attitude has driven almost every single one of my boyfriends nuts. Especially when the meals I've made haven't turned out as expected. Or, more specifically, when the meals I've made haven't turned out as *they* expected. I don't usually have expectations, except for the fact that I want to be nourished and filled to the brim with life force and qi.

I also require certain textures in my mouth, like iceberg lettuce, and peanut butter, and cold, crisp, dark chocolate, and spongy tofu, and thick avocado. Taste is of less importance.

However, this has not been the case for most of my boyfriends or for my father. Taste was a status symbol for them. One boyfriend would roll mouthfuls of food around in his mouth and then spit them out if there was a touch too much turmeric, or pepper, or chili, or paprika, or not enough salt.

Dad always peered over my shoulder as I was preparing meals and would offer a running commentary of what he saw, and what might better it, and what else I should use in it. The kitchen was his domain. He did most of the cooking and the market shopping, while occasionally Mum did the supermarket shopping. Every couple of weeks, she'd make her famous Vietnamese curry. It was the only dish she ever made, because it was the only dish that came out exactly the same every time.

Whenever she experimented with new recipes, or flavors, she'd get really worked up, and flustered, and red in the face. Then Dad would come in and "fix it," and quickly go out and buy her prescription medication from the chemist so that she could take it at bedtime, because, "a headache is definitely coming on." One time she tried to make spanakopita from scratch and she was in bed for a week afterward.

Dad saw his time in the kitchen as relief from work, and yet he never seemed relieved. It was always very high stakes. It was about meeting the needs of recipes, and of other people, and ensuring that everything in the pantry, and in the fridge, and on the spice rack, was fully stocked, and consumed before it went off.

The kitchen was more like a military operation than a space

for relaxation. "Waste not, want not!" he'd chant. "It's just as much of a waste inside of me as it is on the plate if I don't want it or feel like eating it!" I'd chant back. He saw this as a very privileged position, which it was. Although, the fact that people are starving and dying of thirst all around the world has nothing to do with whether or not I eat all of my mashed potato, and everything to do with the fact that billions of us are refusing to build infrastructure that can distribute the earth's resources lovingly and mindfully.

Anyway. Every day before school, Dad would toast me a blueberry bagel and pack my lunch box with, like, leftover pesto pasta and seasonal fruit salad. He saw himself as the Leftover King, and he would plan all of our meals, and the ways in which the leftovers would be divvied up and administered. Not one scrap of food went unaccounted for.

Even when I wanted to start making my own breakfasts and packing my own lunches, he kept offering to do it for me. He'd get up really early and be in the kitchen reading the newspaper and having a cup of tea when I was making my meals. He'd ask me what I wanted from the market, and what I was up to that day, and how I had slept, and he'd want to hug before I was ready to, and then he would forget to buy whatever I'd asked for from the market, and he would say that it was too difficult, and that he couldn't carry it, and, I mean, I needed to write it on the list, and not just tell him about it, and I'd better not ask for cherries again, because they went wrinkly at the back of the fridge that one time, remember?

Then I'd rock up at school with something that I had

put together—maybe a banana and a crunchy peanut butter sandwich—and my friends would look at me, puzzled, and be like, "Geez, just let your dad do it! You're being ridiculous! It's so sweet of him! I wish my dad would make my lunches! My dad never sets foot in the kitchen!"

Dad lives on in this kitchen. He and I are united here through time and space. I'll always be aware of the fact that he doesn't enjoy plant-based cheese, or the addition of coriander because, to him, the taste of cilantro is "too overpowering for any dish." My sprinkling of Himalayan rock salt over the top of the toasted, hardened, buttery bread would be detrimental to his health, and he would brush it off. The mess that I'm going to leave on the kitchen counter wouldn't please him, either. Leaving dishes until the morning irritated him, and he'd always get to them before I had a chance to, and then he'd bitch about it to Mum.

She'd really like this sandwich. Although, she'd never have made it for herself. And even if I had been making these sandwiches every day, she wouldn't have eaten them. She'd have opted for eating the sandwiches that Dad made, with the ingredients that he chose to provide.

49.

I just have to go out and get the coriander, I'll be right back."

"Oh, can I come?"

"Ok."

"I was wondering what lay beyond that window. I could only see my reflection in it before and... there's a pool. Of course there's a pool. I can see your altar from here, too. It's gleaming."

"Yeah, you can see it from quite a few positions around the property. I put it there for that reason. It's also on this energy-meridian-ley-line thing or something."

"More thunder."

"Hmm."

"Porkchop doesn't seem too fazed?"

"No. He's freakishly calm in a storm."

"I wonder what time it is?"

"Yeah."

"You have so many herbs."

"I know. There's a vegetable garden and an orchard, too. It takes quite a bit of work to care for them in the heat. They've got screens over them right now, and there isn't any lettuce. Lettuces are the most problematic in the summer, which is why I have store-bought iceberg at the moment. Sorry about that."

"Are the tomatoes from the garden?"

"Yeah. I'd make my own cheese, too, if I could be bothered. I go through phases."

"I get that."

"Do you garden?"

"Ah. Yeah."

"Smell this."

"Lovely."

"I adore how all of these know how to grow without getting in their own way. They just reach for life around all of the rocks, and all of the challenges. Nothing can stop them. They just give themselves to the world. It's so . . . easy in nature."

"Totally."

"Hmm."

"Do you want me to shut that door?"

"No, no, it's ok. Leave it open."

"Can I be honest with you about something?"

"Sure."

"I, umm. Find this place really sad. Can I say that? I obviously haven't seen all of the rooms or anything. There's just a feeling about it. You've done beautiful things to it. I just . . . yeah."

"If you didn't know what had happened to my family, would you feel the same way?"

"I dunno."

"Hmm."

"I think so?"

"Ok."

"Porkchop's following me."

"Keep your friends close and your enemies closer."

50.

"Ok, we're ready. Want to take your sanga?"

"Sure. Yum."

"Hmm."

"Have you read all of these books?"

"Most of them."

"Really?"

"Yeah. Books are my third parent."

"True."

"Why don't you sit in the big chair?"

"Was that your dad's?"

"No, no. He would've hated that thing. His reading chair is in another room. I bought that one a couple of Christmases ago."

"It's beautiful."

"Thank you."

"I don't think I've seen many round chairs? Or couches?"

"It's a snuggle chair."

"Really?"

"Yep."

"Oh my. I'm not sure I'll ever want to get out of it?"

"Probably not."

"I don't want to stain it?"

"I don't mind."

"Oh, no. Porkchop beat me to it!"

"Man of the house. You can sit with him, though, if you want?"

"Way too intimidating. So what did your dad do?"

"He was an academic."

"Did he write books?"

"Yeah. I still receive royalties from them and stuff. They're pretty highly regarded in academic circles, apparently. I can show them to you if you want. They're in another room. I haven't read them. So. I don't have much to... say about them."

"Right? Why not?"

"Umm. Growing up I always imagined that I'd read them once Mum and Dad had died. And I imagined them dying... you know. Like, later on. When I saw myself reading their work, I was older and I had lived my own life and developed my own ideas about things. There was a stronger sense of distance between me and them, or something. I didn't see myself as reading their work now. It seems too soon."

"Would I have heard of them?"

"I doubt it."

"Ok. I'd better stop talking now and have a bite of this. It looks amazing. I'm not entirely used to plant-based sandwiches. I'm excited, though."

"Ok."

"Mmm."

"Yeah?"

"Shit, yeah. Thank you. Fucking *yum*."

"Yay."

Ok, so eating is one of the most exposing and vulnerable acts you can witness a person participating in. How they interact with nourishing themselves reveals how they interact with life.

He takes big mouthfuls and savors each one. He goes out of his way to get a little bit of every ingredient into his gob in one go. Then, he closes his eyes, and experiences it, passionately, before plunging in and taking another voluminous bite and going through the motions all over again. He doesn't try to make the sandwich more contained via nibbling at its edges, or quickly catching blobs of avocado in his mouth as they cascade out the bottom. He lets them fall, before picking them up with his oily fingers and adding them to the mouthful that he's currently chewing.

When I was in high school, girls in my year level told me that it was best not to eat in front of boys. Even if the plan was to go out for food together, it was preferable to opt for a smoothie, or a milkshake, or a juice, or a coffee. So they'd sip their dainty drinks and smile as their companions ate with their mouths open, and talked and laughed their way through chicken parmas, and burgers, and chips, and fizzy drinks.

One girl who had been in a relationship for almost eight months was adamant that her boyfriend had never, ever, seen her eat—and she was very proud of this. I asked them if they ever took shits at their boyfriends' houses and they looked at me as if I was an evil goblin out to get them, because I was.

I've always eaten in front of boys and men, and I've always taken dumps at their houses. Both activities are basic human rights. When you've gotta eat, you've gotta eat, and when you've gotta go, you've gotta go. Wearing a corset isn't in fashion anymore so I'm not about to use dieting, or restriction, in its place.

However, I do enjoy eating slowly and steadily. I don't like too many ingredients falling out of a sandwich, either. That annoys me. I want to taste everything, in small mouthfuls. I want to be in control, and fully conscious as I eat. Yet, sometimes, the social situation surrounding the act of eating overwhelms me, and I find myself eating mindlessly or I need to stop eating altogether.

"I'm going to polish this off pretty fucking fast."

"I wish I'd made you another?"

"No, no. One is perfect."

"Ok. Well, I don't think I can finish this. You can have it if you want?"

"You sure?"

"Yeah, yeah, please. I'm kind of tired. Would you be up for sleeping?"

"Yeah."

"Like, actually sleeping. I could put you in one of the spare rooms, or you could sleep with me. I just...when I say I need sleep, I mean it. I don't mean sex, and I don't mean fooling around. I'm too tired. Is that ok?"

"Yeah, I get it."

"Sorry, you're just having your last mouthful."

"No, no, all done—right with you. Delicious. Seriously. Thank you."

"My pleasure. Are you ok in the dark? I can't be bothered turning the lights on."

"Yep, yep. Oops! Are these the stairs?"

"Yep, we're going upstairs."

"Ok."

"Here."

His hands are so elegant and yet so unexpectedly clammy, and callus-y. I read in a book by Louise Hay that calluses are to do with our ideas and fears solidifying or something. Although, a psychic once said to me that I developed them because I'm holding on to the world too tightly. She saw my calluses as a strong desire to stay here, and to survive.

We're almost at my room, and I'm making a conscious effort to walk slowly, because I love holding hands. Only one boyfriend has ever really held my hand, and it was when we were crossing the road, as if I was his little girl and he was my daddy. Most of my boyfriends have put their arms around my shoulders when we're walking down the street, which has sometimes felt too heavy and cumbersome. Then, at other times, the weight of them has felt calming and reassuring. My last boyfriend shared with me that when he put his arm around me, it wasn't for me. It was for him when he was feeling scared, and unsteady.

"What a room."

"Yeah."

"I'm not sure I've ever slept in a four-poster bed?"

"I'm going to open the balcony doors so that we can hear the rain when it comes and then I'm going to pass out. I can already smell it. Mmm. Do you need anything?"

"No, no. I'm good."

"Cool."

"I just realized how tired I am."

"Lightning."

"Yeah."

"Whoa."

"Goodnight, then."

"Goodnight."

51.

I just dreamed about him. We were sitting at the party again and we were talking, and it was exactly the same as before, except there was a cliff next to us, which dropped directly into the ocean. The sky was bright blue, and there were waves crashing at the bottom of the massive decline. I could feel the spray from it on my face. He didn't seem to notice or to be bothered by it. So we kept talking and talking. Then, all of a sudden, he became distracted and stood up, and turned around, and lost his balance, and slipped, and I reached out, and caught him with my left hand, and it wasn't too difficult for me to hold on to him. He was just hanging there, and he goes, "Let me fall, let me fall," and I was like, "Are you sure? I can hold on to you?" and he said, "I need to fall, I need to fall." So I let him.

52.

He's crashed into my room like a spaceship. He doesn't snore, although he's clearly sleeping very deeply. Maybe that's the effect of the alcohol. I might stroke his hair and see if he stirs. Nope. Nothing. Very still.

He has this effortless quality about him, which is a bit worrying. I wonder if he's ever truly hit the bottom of any feeling. I can imagine that there's always been someone or something to distract him from himself. Like, he's drifted a bit, and floated about without realizing it, and now he anchors himself through sleep.

He'd be the kind of guy to engage in a stimulating discussion, or some sort of tragedy would occur in his family, or someone at work would upset him, and he'd have to go to sleep immediately. I'm the opposite. I can't sleep unless I feel safe. I'm surprised that I managed it just now.

The sun has risen, and it's raining outside. I love his shoulders. They're enormous. They'd probably threaten other men.

I bet he's been teased and bullied a lot because of the size of his shoulders. He has a big heart, too, which most people can't handle. People think that courage isn't inherent, and that it must be worked for and earned. So those who exhibit effortless strength, and love, become dangerous and untrustworthy. Then, the only way to reclaim power in their presence is to try to take theirs away from them.

I once read a story about a man who traveled to a village. He wanted to get to know the people living there and their ways of life. He was working in the fields when all of the villagers started screaming and running, and he turned around and saw that they were running from a watermelon.

So he went up to the watermelon and held it between his hands and lifted it up to them and said, "It's just a watermelon!" They all stopped and looked at him in horror. Then he put the watermelon down and sliced it up into pieces, and went, "See, you can even eat it. It's delicious. Look!" He shoved some watermelon into his mouth, and chewed it, and swallowed it, and relished in every last piece of it, and allowed its juices to pour down his chin. "See?"

The villagers swarmed upon him, and tied him up, and nailed him to a crucifix, and tortured him over the course of three days until he died.

Another man arrived at the village and wanted to get to know the people living there and their ways of life. He was working in the fields when all of the villagers started screaming and running. He turned around and saw that they were running from a watermelon, and he thought it was ridiculous.

I mean, it was just a fucking watermelon. Nevertheless, he decided to run and scream, too.

He spent years running and screaming alongside all of the villagers. He even started an anti-watermelon campaign and declared war upon the watermelons. All of the people in the village adored him, and looked up to him, and were so thankful for the protection and care that he provided for them.

53.

His hair is quite oily. He mustn't wash it much. It's like his dirty little secret. His one indulgence in depravity. He smells a bit, too. Smoky and sweet near his armpits. The rain just got heavier. I always miss the rain when I'm not dancing in it.

It's so weird when people don't go outside to enjoy the rain, or to see a rainbow when it appears, because they're "in the middle of something." It's like, I'm sorry? Do you have better things to do? Like, what better things are there to do? What pressing or urgent matters could there possibly be to attend to? It's fucking raining! There might be a fucking rainbow! Beings from other planets and dimensions would do anything to be a part of this and to witness this shit! Get outside, dammit!

"Hmm."

"Hmm?"

"Hey."

"It's raining."

"Yeah."

"I love that sound."

"Me too."

"Did you sleep?"

"A bit, I think."

"You seem really awake."

"Do I?"

"Yeah. Are you a light sleeper?"

"Maybe."

"Definitely."

"I think I want to go outside."

"Outside?"

"Yeah."

"Into the rain?"

"Yeah."

"Ok?"

"Do you want to come?"

"Umm. Not really? I'm not sure. What are you going to do out there?"

"Be... in the rain."

"Right. Umm."

"It's ok. You keep sleeping. I'll be back."

54.

The rain is getting heavier, and I can't get down the stairs fast enough. He hasn't followed me, and I get it. No guy has ever followed me into the rain. They've always kept watching the basketball on TV, or they've gone back to sleep, because it's "too much" and I'm being a "freak." Dancing in the rain doesn't "make sense" and it doesn't have a specific "outcome." Well, it does, it's just that the physical outcome tends to involve being wet, and cold, and needing to go inside, and get warm, and have a shower, and maybe have a cup of tea, which is part of what I like about it.

Porkchop is already sitting at the bottom of the stairs in anticipation, and when he saw me he flopped onto his back and started squirming and rolling around on the marble in excitement.

I'm glad I left the kitchen door open. Now I can just throw the kimono off, and fly out, into the rain. Wow. There are some seriously big, cold drops smashing against my skin. They're so tropical and uncompromising. I'm getting waves of chills. I have to consciously, like, relax the muscles in my neck and jaw and arms.

I really want to go down onto the lawn, although he might not be able to find me if he needs me? Oh, well. He could probably see me from the veranda. I'm going to go and lie down on the grass and roll in the mud. Fuck me. I lie on this lawn every day and it always feels different. The rain is pounding me into it, deeper and deeper, and the earth is moving, and I don't know how I'm going to clean myself up without making a mess all over the house. Oh, well.

"Oi!"

"Oh!"

"Do you need a towel?"

"Umm, not right now?"

"Where are the towels?"

"What?"

"Where are the towels? I'll put one out here! On the deck!"

"Ok? The towels are in the bathroom! Downstairs! Kind of behind the kitchen!"

"Ok!"

I wonder what he's going to do once he has finished the task that he has created for himself.

"Here it is!"

"What?"

"I've put it here!"

"Ok?"

"It's gotten so heavy!"

"What?"

"The rain!"

"Yeah!"

"Yeah!"

"It's gotten so heavy!"

"I know!"

"What are you doing?"

"What d'you mean?"

"Umm!"

"Do you want to come down?"

"I don't know!"

"Ok!"

"Should I?"

"I don't know!"

"Fuck it! I'm coming down!"

"Really! Shit!"

"Yes! Really!"

"Look at you! Tearing off those pesky clothes!"

"Rahh!"

"Rahh!"

"Whoa! It's so slippery! Shit! Almost fucking died just then!"

"Look."

"You're really getting into it."

"It feels amazing. It's so good for your skin."

"Fuck! That does feel good. It's so long since I've...felt mud. I'm not sure I've ever been able to, like, roll in it. Not even as a kid, I don't think?"

"What?"

"I love the mud!"

"I know!"

His body is one of the most beautiful things I've ever seen. He's looking at me now and a switch has gone off, or on, or something. I know that look. Yet it's also a new look, because it's coming from him. The rain suits him.

He just lay down next to me and put his hand on my stomach and he's pressing it. Now it's on my heart and wrapping itself around my neck. He's brushed hair off my face, and everything is turning to mud and water. His hand is moving back down to my thighs, and he's squeezing them, and his body is close enough to my body for me to be able to feel that he's hard. I'm so happy not to be speaking. His dick is so insistent. I laughed and he didn't hear, I don't think, which is probably for the best.

He's holding my tits with both hands, and kissing them, and sucking my nipples. Not with any teeth, though, which is nice. I hate it when the teeth come into play too soon and shock me out of feeling safe, and sensual, and soft. It's just his lips and tongue. I've put my hands on his chest, and the hair is coarse, and curly, and tangled. He's like a big, wet love heart. Such narrow hips! I didn't realize how narrow his hips were. I just squeezed his bum. It's so tense! There's so much tightness in his bum. His shoulders have become all shiny, and slippery, and sinewy. I can taste bits of dirt in my mouth, and they're crunchy.

I don't want to have sex and I think he knows that. His hand is on my face, and I've taken his thumb into my mouth. Oh, his body, and his dick, and the fucking rain, and sucking on his fucking thumb. I'm going to close my eyes. Oh, no. His hand just went to my vagina. I clenched my thighs and he got the message and retreated. This is enough. This is . . . so much.

His eyes are tiny and squinty under the weight of the rain. His hair is falling in front of his face, and I want to kiss. I want to be in contact with everything that is precious about being a human being. There's no hiding behind a kiss. During a really good kiss, there are no power struggles. It's making out with humanness. It's heaven on earth. It's eyes open, and closed, and lips, and breath, and flesh, and stubble. Hopefully not enough to enter into rash territory. Just enough to be conscious of the fact that, yes, hair grows on this person's face and, yes, he shaves it occasionally, and the last time he might have done so was about a week to ten days ago.

I love it when kisses twist and turn like this one. We're a winding path, reading each other's minds, and chasing each other's faces. There are no knots. We're coming undone. His hands are kissing the sides of my face, and neck, and hair, and the length of my arms, and he's lifting up my lower back, and the lips of my vagina are swelling every time the length of his body presses against mine.

Not having sex can be so sexy. Now I'm curious about what it would feel like to have his hands in, and on, my vagina. I'm wondering about what it would be like to have his mouth on my vagina, and his penis inside of it, and our stomachs pressing together, and our thighs crushing at all different angles, and his hands grabbing and clenching at my arse cheeks, and at my stomach, and at my hips, and at my waist, and up, and down, and on top, and on the bottom, and all around, and everything. His lips are so full and plump, which is surprising. They don't look as sumptuous as they feel.

Now I'm remembering this hot-yoga class I went to where the instructor walked around the room as we were doing downward dog and kept repeating, "It's magic, it's magic," with a heavy Russian accent. "It's magic, it's magic."

I'm so glad we didn't kiss until it was right to kiss. Like, at the point when we couldn't *not* kiss. We've gotten into such a rhythm. It's become so relaxing.

He just poked his tongue into my mouth, and I poked mine back. He smiled, and I know that he did, because I felt his teeth. I've just wrapped my hand around his dick, and squeezed it. He moved his thighs slightly apart, so I put one hand around his balls, and tugged them. They're perfect, and the weight of his thighs is so comforting.

I don't want to go any further. I don't want his dick inside of me. There's so much stimulation and nourishment already occurring. A dick in my vagina would subtract from that somehow. It would pierce the moment, rather than add to it. I'm a process, not an object, you know? Don't just shove things in me. A man's energy stays inside a woman's body for up to a year, so. You know. It's not something to be taken lightly.

My hand has fallen into quite a fluid and intuitive movement around his penis. I'm barely thinking about it. It's at a bit of a strange angle. Although, I think that it must be putting pressure on all of the most tender and sensitive parts, because he's quivering and losing concentration on the kissing. I'm crying, although the rain would conceal that from him.

I've often cried during sex. One guy was really into having rough intercourse, and my body would involuntarily weep at its commencement. Like, before I even had time to realize what was happening, I was wailing.

One night he was fucking me from behind and it seemed to be more sensual and sensitive than usual, and I remember noticing this, and feeling surprised and relieved, and then he thrust his penis into my arsehole, and I shrieked, and jolted forward, and I was shaking for hours afterward.

I mean, a dick is not a gun. It's not a machine. It's flesh. It's relatively harmless. Yet the sense of intrusion, and invasion, was palpable. My arsehole ached for days and my mind reeled around the incident for years. He said that he felt terrible, and that I was clearly just "less confident" and "less experienced" in the bedroom than he was.

I've released my hand slightly and his forehead is now resting against mine. Maybe he sensed that I was crying? I'm not sure.

Another boyfriend hated it when I cried with joy during sex because he couldn't do the same. It made him feel less divine, and upon realizing that I was crying, and that I loved him, he'd roll over, sigh, stand up, put on a T-shirt, and walk out of the room.

The rain is easing. I wonder if he wants to orgasm? He's still hard. I might just tickle his penis a bit with my fingertips as we lie here. Actually, I might rub it all over myself first. It's pulsating with so much energy and power. Apparently, putting a hard dick on your forehead is one of the best remedies for a headache.

The sky is so bright, and white, and the glare is super-intense. Oh, shit, he's coming! When the rain comes, so does everything. His stomach is undulating, and his quads are tightening, and his eyes are shut, and his head has turned away, and the veins in his arms and neck have become pronounced, like powerful little rivers. He looks like he's about to die.

"I'm sorry."

"Why?"

"You didn't get to come."

"Oh, no. Don't do that."

"I'm exhausted."

"Yeah."

"Is it the middle of the day? Or?"

"It must be the afternoon by now."

"Really?"

"Yeah."

"Ok."

"Hmm."

"I'd . . . better get to my parents' soon."

"To help your mum with the Christmas cooking?"

"Yeah."

"And her famous guac."

"Yeah."

"Do you want to have a shower before you leave or something?"

"Sure, yeah, that'd be good."

"Ok."

"The sun's coming out."

"Hmm."

I can feel his heartbeat slowing. The dirt is drying and caking to my body. My skin feels like it's pulling at itself. He only brought one towel out onto the veranda and now I'm having déjà vu. Fuck. I'm looking over and seeing Porkchop sitting at the door and it's not the first time. It's not the first time, nor is it the only time, or the last time. This has happened many, many times, and it will continue to happen again, and again, over and over, into infinity.

We're going to have to share the towel. I might run inside and get my own. He only grabbed a mini-sized one from the bathroom for some reason, so our ability to hold each other inside of it is distinctly limited. Although, he seems a bit distant, anyway. He probably needs space, which I can understand. Ejaculation takes a lot out of a guy. I almost feel bad about it. The idea of it seems pleasurable, and in the moment it can seem like a release, and then they lose so much life force.

Now his body is attempting to recover and muster up some energy again. I wonder if he ejaculates regularly, or how long it's been since he last did. Some men come all of the time, and others look like if they came too much, or too regularly, they'd keel over and be unable to function.

"I'm just going to go inside and get another towel."

"Oh, ok, sorry?"

"That's ok. I'll just be a sec."

"I'll follow you."

"Ok."

"Hey? What's in there?"

"Oh. That's my parents' bedroom."

"The door was open, I didn't mean to—"

"The wind must've opened it."

"Oh."

"Did you . . ."

"No, no."

"I can show you, if you want?"

"No. Truly."

"It's fine. Come in."

"Is this . . . how they left it?"

"Yeah."

"Holy shit."

"There's a chair just behind you."

"Ok, thanks. Umm. Fuck, sorry, I got dirt on it!"

"Don't worry about it."

"Sorry. Go and get yourself a towel or whatever?"

"Ok. Are you going to be all right if I leave you in here for a sec?"

"Yeah, yeah."

"Ok."

55.

Oh, no. This can't be good. He's literally sitting in my parents' bedroom, naked, covered in dirt. I hope I don't faint. Once, after a third date, I was so overcome with receiving focused, positive attention from someone else that I swooned on the bathroom floor in the middle of the night. I went to the toilet, looked in the mirror, and woke up on the tiles with huge, bleeding scratches across my back from where I had hit the edge of the cabinet as I plummeted downward.

"So, why is it... like this? Why is their room still like this?"

"Umm. Well. I emptied most of the house when they died. I burned a lot of stuff, and I gave a lot to charity and to different archives. The only rooms I've left the same are this one and Dad's writing room. All of the others are empty, or I've turned them into spaces that have new meaning for me. The

Christmas presents I get for myself each year fill the rooms with new things. This door is usually shut. So. Yeah."

"Fuck."

"Hmm."

"The bedside clock is broken?"

"Yeah."

"Death is . . . weird."

"Hmm."

"The way people just . . . vanish. And, like, leave shit behind. It's creepy."

"I know. I often think about it in terms of aliens. Like, we appear on this planet, and then we just . . . disappear. Poof. We can't be explained. It's funny how we wonder about whether or not aliens exist and, you know. All we need to do is look in the mirror. Like, hello. Here we are."

"Trippy."

"Hmm."

"Can I see some other rooms?"

"Really?"

"Yeah."

"Are you sure?"

"Yeah."

"Now?"

"Yeah. Is that ok?"

"Umm."

"Not all of them, or anything. Just... one that might... I don't know. Leave with me a different impression. This one is... intense."

"Ok."

"Yeah?"

"Yeah. I know the one. Follow me."

56.

I'm going to take him into the room behind the living room. The doorway to it is concealed by the Christmas tree. Although, no one has ever really noticed the door before. They've never had the sense that they're missing out on anything. Usually, after encountering the rose garden, and the altar, and the fountain, people are sufficiently inundated and ready to leave. Or they just want to watch TV, and lie by the pool, and get food delivered.

No one has ever seen my parents' bedroom, either. Nor have they ever rolled around in the mud or the rain with me. Given that, I feel compelled to offer him access to the room behind the living room, if he wants it. I had it built the first Christmas after Mum and Dad died. It takes quite a bit to maintain, and I suspect that's why I had it constructed. It provided a very wholesome distraction.

The room itself is heavily insulated and it emulates the tropical climate of North Queensland. I go in there almost every morning and water down all of the plants, and check the temperature, and make adjustments if necessary. In the summer it's easier to keep at about eighty-five degrees, because it's so hot outside. Then, each night, I let it cool down a bit. Not too much. The humidity is always around sixty to seventy percent.

All four walls of the room—and the floor and the door—are painted yellow. The ceiling is made of thick glass. The room is filled with hot-pink *Pentas* plants, and bright-orange *Ixora* flowers, and fluffy *Melicopes*, and *Euodia* trees. There are some voluptuous ice-cream bean trees and pagoda plants, too, and the mistletoe is going cray-cray right now. As are the figs. I must remember to pick some. Figs are very sexy. There are also quite a few juicy little white mulberries emerging, and the leaves of the basswood are at their darkest and deepest green. It's actually the perfect time for him to be seeing the room.

"I didn't notice that door?"

"No."

"Is Porkchop allowed in?"

"Ah, no. Off you go, mate. Ok. So. You might get a shock at first. Umm. There's nothing in here that can harm you, ok?"

"Ok?"

"And I'll stay with you for a bit and then I'll leave, maybe? That way, you can have time in there to yourself. I'll come in at the start, so you know that it's safe. Kind of like in medieval England when both people would drink the wine at dinner just to be sure that the other hadn't put poison in it or something."

"Right."

"Ok."

"Ok. What do I do with my towel?"

"Leave it on. Or take it off. Whatever."

"Ok. Ok."

"Here we go."

57.

The first time I went to the Melbourne Zoo with my parents and they took me into the Butterfly House, I knew that the end was nigh upon us. The unpredictability, and swooping, and flittering about, and transience, and innocence, and slime, and speed, and squirming, and sap—it was all too much for me.

And I was shocked and appalled by how calm my mother was. Especially given her attitude toward insects in general. She was always asking Dad to kill spiders around the house and spraying insecticide everywhere.

So I flipped out and chose to wait at the exit for them. The prospect of one of those loose little cretins landing on me, and smacking its body parts against my face, and flitting off at its leisure wasn't what I had in mind when visiting the zoo.

I thought that I was going to be placed safely behind railings and outside of lions' cages. I thought that I'd be able to stand behind immense walls of Perspex in order to look at the fish and the seals. I didn't expect to be in the thick of it: fending for myself among the people, and the insects, and the animals.

Because when you're in the presence of butterflies, you have to keep your body still, and your mind open, and I wasn't ready for that. I was terrified of killing one of them, or of becoming so excited at the prospect of one of them landing upon my hand, or my arm, that I would clasp at it, and crush it, and harm it irreparably. I couldn't bear their fragility. I couldn't trust myself with it.

58.

A Ulysses just went straight for his face, and then for his shoulder, and now it's just sitting there, electric blue and calm. He didn't even flinch. It's loving the dirt on his skin. It must be the perfect mix of saltiness and grime.

I had to get a license to breed the Ulysses and his female counterparts. It wasn't hard. Scientists and researchers and breeders occasionally come by and visit, and I make them black coffee, without milk, and they take notes, and carry various samples back to different corners of the country in order to help support the butterflies' native habitats, and their sanctuaries.

A while ago, there was a fear that the Ulysses was dying out. So I used the opportunity that my grief presented to help create this little world for them. I don't use herbicides or insecticides, because it harms their growth and disrupts their food sources. There are also a lot of ants. They love the butterflies. They protect their cocoons, and various stages of development, and metamorphosis. Apparently, the butterflies release some sort of sugar, or acid, or whatever, and the ants adore it. They can't get enough. So I don't want to harm them.

The Ulysses is also known as the Blue Mountain Swallowtail, and it can live from a week to up to a year. Larger butterflies live a lot longer than smaller ones. They're also coldblooded, which means that they can't regulate their own temperatures. So if the room falls below eighty-two degrees, they won't be able to fly, or eat, or mate. The ceiling is made of thick glass in order to keep it warm. They like to bask in the sunshine and open up their enormous, four-to-five-inch-wide blue-and-black wings, and hurry about with excitement, or sit motionless, allowing their tiny veins to fill with heat and blood before moving around again.

Sometimes they just perch on a leaf, and open and close their wings slowly and steadily, as if they're thinking very deeply. They fly at speeds of up to 12 miles per hour and it can take some time to get used to them, and to their pace, and to being approached, and touched, and chosen by them. They're quite insistent, in their way. With each other, and with everyone, and everything.

He's handling it well, though. He instinctively knows to move slowly, and now there are at least ten butterflies dancing around his body, and casually moving from arm to arm, and leg to leg, to atop his head, and onto his shoulders, and off again.

Aristotle called butterflies Psyche, which is the Greek word for soul. The myth of Cupid and Psyche was one of my favorite bedtime stories as a child. Although, when I came upon a mythology book that was less oriented around sugar-coating things for children and parents, and more inclined toward grappling with suffering, and malevolence, I learned that the myth of Cupid and Psyche could be super-brutal. Like, Psyche had some serious suicidal ideation issues.

And in many cultures, butterflies are seen to bridge the world of the living with the world of the dead. The Aztecs believed that the spirits of happy deceased relatives visited those who were still alive in the form of butterflies.

59.

Oh, wow. A female Ulysses just landed on his forehead. He's shut his eyes. Very wise. Surrender, and let her do her thing. The first time she landed on me, I entered a portal and never came out. I'm still in it, I think.

She has little crescent moons on her wings, which differentiate her from the male. She's so enormous, and gentle. During our first encounter, she landed on the top of my left hand, and I had to consciously keep breathing and keep my limbs supple as she tested my skin and got to know me.

She told me about how people think the world revolves around them, and that it's very funny. As she sat on my wrist, I looked around the room and realized how quiet it was. I had never noticed before. I mean, I'd often watched the butterflies dancing around each other, and feverishly interacting, and fluttering apart, and finding one another again, higher up, and closer to the glass. Yet their silence hadn't dawned upon me.

"Holy shit."

"Hmm."

"I wish I could . . . see what you see."

"I wish I could see what you see."

"Come here."

He's crying, and I don't know why, and I'm not going to ask, because it doesn't matter. He wants to be held and I can do that. That's what matters. I can hold him, and then I can let him go.

60.

I decided to wear a silk dressing gown and slippers to the door because I wanted him to see me in a silk dressing gown and slippers at the door. I tried to smile and it felt like it was overdoing things a bit, so I restrained myself. I even considered chasing after him because I liked the idea of being able to do that. Yet the fact that I considered chasing after him at all caused me to be embarrassed at myself, so I decided to ditch gestures that were at one time used to control something that cannot be controlled. Smiling at or chasing a person can't change the reality of what a good-bye is or the way that it's felt for, like, centuries. Eons, even. So let a good-bye be a good-bye, and my life on earth can be whatever it is, too.

Acknowledgments

I would like to thank the following people and animals for the roles that they've played in my life, and in the writing, editing, and publishing of this book: Kristina Andersen, Sofia Andersen, Paul Cox, Casey Denis, Ellen Dutton, Debi Enker, Mala Enker, Ashlen Francisco, Jess Grose, Heather Karpas, Katinka, Sharon Krum, Mary MacKenzie, Sharne McGee, Rabbi, Andrew Rule, Tom Ryan, Zoe Swanton, Alissa Tanskaya, Danielle Teutsch, Totoro, Marika Webb-Pullman, Michal de Willoughby, Fiona Wood, Zero, and Barbara Zitwer.

And I'm especially grateful for the contributions of Hector H. MacKenzie, who held *A Room Called Earth* in his heart and mind through every stage of its development.